We Can't Go Home Again

Max Andrew Dubinsky

"The Boy With His Heart On His Sleeve and the Girl Who Never Tried To Fix Him" originally appeared on *dailylove.net* in 2010. "We Can't Go Home Again" originally appeared on *MakeItMAD.com* in 2010.

The digital edition of this book was published in 2011 by BookBaby.

We Can't Go Home Again

ISBN-13: 978-1470087715

PRAISE FOR

WE CAN'T GO HOME AGAIN

"[Dubinsky] paints a poignant story of redemption, forgiveness, and home. He provides an avenue of sober self-examination and exploration...navigating through shades of gray as he takes you on a journey of honest, raw healing. A must read."

-Ashley Smith,
People of the Second Chance

"Dubinsky is a natural storyteller. And like any great bard, Max appeals to our whole selves -- the broken, bitter, and beautiful. His voice is honest and unassuming. These heartfelt stories are full of humanity and sure to make you remember home -- a place full of laughter, tears, and healing."

-Jeff Goins,
Goinswriter.com

"*We Can't Go Home Again* is a uniquely told process of discovery, painting a landscape of human angst and pain in search of redemption. Dubinsky has a unique way of capturing the inner world of a tortured soul by telling their outward story. His minimalist approach to writing allows the reader to search for and find himself in the staccato style dialogue and storylines. I couldn't put these stories down, and in turn, these stories never let me down."

-Bob Hamp,
author of *Think Differently, Live Differently*

"As I read *We Can't Go Home Again,* I did so gripped to the pages and at times with tears streaming down my face. With a dark rawness and a ribbon of hope throughout, Max writes the stories of individuals I could have known. Or even could have become. A quick and yet poignant must read."

-Crystal Renaud,
author of *Dirty Girls Come Clean*

For Lauren.

This book happened because of you. Thank you for dragging out the fiction writer you saw inside me, and believing the world would want to see him too.

&

For Julianne Gulu.

Thank you for reading every word I have ever written.

CONTENTS

ACKNOWLEDGEMENTS

Thank you, God, for my ability to write and screw up repeatedly in this life so that I may have this opportunity to give the world a glimpse through fiction what your endless grace and forgiveness look like.

Sally Dubinsky, you've been my biggest fan from the very beginning. You read what I wrote even when you disagreed with it. You shared my work, listened to my crazy ideas, let me drop out of college, and even showed up to my wedding when I eloped with a girl on a cliff in Denver. You raised me to be the man I have become today, Mom, and I will love you forever.

Haley Cloyd, you offered me a roof over my head, endless encouragement, gluten-free ideas, friendship, and if that wasn't enough, you even took the time to proofread these stories. Thank you.

Jesse McClain, you found the writer inside of me back in seventh grade using poetry, the Holocaust, and *The Twilight Zone* to successfully lure him out. I'm not sure these stories would be in the world today if it wasn't for you.

And to the readers of Make It MAD, thank you for following my story, taking me in while I lived on the road, and being a part of the adventure. Your faith in this world and in God restored mine. This book is for you guys.

THE BOY WITH HIS HEART ON HIS SLEEVE AND THE GIRL WHO NEVER TRIED TO FIX HIM

I was born with my heart on my sleeve. Despite popular belief, there were no complications in the delivery room. When the doctor handed me over to my mother, he told her to be careful.

"He's fragile," he said.

Mom cried when she held me for the first time, overjoyed at the prospect of raising a son who would be so in touch with his emotions. Maybe I wouldn't be like all the other men in her life.

Dad sat in the corner, shaking his head, already disappointed in me like I had any say in the matter. Like I wanted to be born this way.

"It's not all that uncommon of an affliction," the doctor tried to reassure him. "A lot of men carry their hearts on their sleeves."

"I think he's beautiful," Mom said, tears still in her eyes.

When Dad had his buddies over from work for the big game

the following Sunday, they stood around my crib shaking their heads and consoling him with pats on the back, clinking beer bottles together.

One friend informed them, "My wife says it's okay for men to be this way. Says the world would be a better place if more men were born like your boy here."

The men only stared.

"My wife," he shrugged, "she reads a lot. Is always getting these crazy ideas. But still..."

"The doctor," Dad told them, "said this isn't that uncommon of an affliction."

Mom hates when people use that word.

Affliction.

I asked her how we should describe my condition then.

"You're just more vulnerable than most," she said with a smile one morning cooking eggs and cinnamon toast.

Just once I'd like not to cry when the sun sets.

In school, the kids knew there was something different about me. I'd show up to class wearing turtle neck sweaters in June.

I cried every morning I got on the bus, leaving Mom behind in the driveway like it was the last time I was ever going to see her. In high school I had no problem dating, but none of the girls took my marriage proposals for serious affairs.

"What about college?" they'd ask. "We've never even been to Europe," they'd say.

"Forget Europe," I'd tell them. "I'm going to college wherever you're going."

But you, you were different. There was something so understanding about you. The day we met, you had your hair pulled back and wore that awful orange jacket you picked up at the Goodwill. I wore a sweater Mom bought me for Christmas. So you didn't know until it got good and hot in that coffee shop, and I rolled up my sleeves. When you saw who I really was, you said you were glad I wasn't like the rest. I asked what you meant. You smiled and said, "Normal is so boring."

You were a machine, and I was just a boy with his heart on his sleeve.

"This has tragedy written all over it," I used to say to you again and again.

You would tell me to stop over-analyzing everything. "Just enjoy the moment."

I was relentless. You were unresponsive.

After you left, I decided to try and see if I could live without it. Without my heart on my sleeve. So I cut it off. And I put in a box.

Then I hid the box.

Where no one could ever get to it.

No one but me.

Eventually, I forgot where I put the box.

Eventually, I stopped thinking about the box, or even wondering what life was like living with a heart.

Everything was far easier.

Then I saw you at the bar with his arm around your waist, your hands in his pockets, his lips on your ear, and I felt nothing but the place where my heart used to be.

I felt it tingle. I felt it crawl. Then I felt nothing at all.

Which was nice. For a while, at least.

Until she came along.

There was something about her. I couldn't quite figure it out. Until she pushed up her sleeves, and I saw the scars.

I asked her where she put it. Where did she put her heart? Did she throw it away or give it as a gift at Christmas?

"I put it in a safe place," she told me. "Where no one could ever get to it."

No one but her.

When she asked why I acted so strange sometimes, I informed her that I couldn't remember where I put my heart. And for the first time in my life I had finally found a use for it.

She smiled.

She offered me hers.

I shook my head. I pleaded with her to take it back.

"I can't accept that."

"I won't know what to do with it."

"It'll only end up bruised, hurt, and worse off than it was before you left it under my care."

She said she was willing to take the risk.

I tore through my closets, my car, my pockets, but still, I could not remember my safe place. I had to give her something in return, but nothing other than my own heart would ever good enough.

Then one evening alone in her apartment, she told me it was okay.

"Your heart," she said, "you gave it to me. I have it. It is safe."

I didn't understand.

I asked her how this was possible.

She looked at me like she couldn't believe I'd even ask such a thing. She wanted my trust. She put her hand on my arm where my heart used to be. She touched my chest where I kept hers, and cared for it as though it were my own.

She said, "You cry every time we watch the sun set."

31 DAYS OF MAY

Day 1.
19 hours sober.

Mom doesn't hug me quite the way she used to. Loose and devastating like I'm some highly infectious disease, she'd have been better off not making any effort at all. Let's at least call this what it is. In her defense, maybe I'm making it awkward by holding my bags, but smart money says it's because she can't quite believe I'm her son. I can't possibly be the child she nursed and whose school lunches she packed. The son with scraped knees she patched up again and again; held when he cried.

I could see it in her eyes if she'd only just look at me.

The front door remains open at my back. Lawnmowers and lawn darts, skateboards and sprinklers. Summer creeps in around us.

Dad stands in the doorway to the kitchen, an unlit cigarette pressed between his lips. He strikes match after match, tossing them into the sink. Each one extinguished before it lands. The house is burnt with nicotine. I go for my pockets and think about lighting one up right here with my old man so we can have some common ground to stand on—for a moment at any rate. I can't believe Mom lets this habit indoors now. To be honest, there's a hell of a lot I can't believe these days. I guess on that long grocery list of things, this is far from significant—Dad smoking in the house now—but it doesn't settle well with me.

Just like Mom's hug.

She tells me I can put my bags in my room. "It's just the way you left it."

"Your hair's getting long."

I look at my father, self-consciously tucking a few stray strands behind my ear. With the next match he finally lights that cigarette. Extinguished, it chases the others into the sink.

"It looks good," Mom says, smiling hard.

I'm a guest in my own goddamn home.

Day 2.

52 hours sober.

The doctors here gave me this journal, and told me to write any time I feel anxious. Any time I feel anything at all.

The coffee here is shit.

That's how I feel about that.

I had a hard time leaving the room today.

Gary—he's been here 72 days and counting—said that's normal. That happens to most of the guys.

Shame.

I wouldn't exactly tell him he's right.

But I'm not going to tell you he's wrong either.

Last night Gary asked if I had a light, and we smoked some twenty-odd cigarettes over coffee.

He asked my age.

He asked if I had a girlfriend.

He asked if I believed in God.

He asked a lot of things.

Gary's 43 and still can't grow a full beard. He looks like hell with his patchy facial hair, and skin that's spent too much time in the sun.

I can't find the energy to believe in someone who doesn't believe in me.

Gary said I'm sorely mistaken. He might be the only one left who believes.

God, that is.

Not Gary.

There are no more photographs. That, and the televisions are gone. As if the sudden disappearance of every family photo ever taken wasn't enough to make me feel unwelcome, there's no longer a television in any room of the house. Or a computer. I guess that's understandable—the computers. My father's laptop is gone, and the family computer downstairs in the living room—the same one Timmy played all his games on—has disappeared too.

But the televisions? They removed every piece of technology in the place, and sent us back to the Stone Age on account of my return.

There's not even a fucking magazine left on the coffee table.

Day 3.

Lynn, you always said you lived without regrets, but is there anyone out there who ever really did it?

Gary wasn't at the meeting today. He said with special cases, guys like him—120 day guys, guys who've been here two, three times—guys like him go to a different kind of meeting. Meetings—he told me tonight over another twenty-seven cigarettes—that I should be more grateful about not attending. I can't imagine it's worse than listening to the fifteen sad-sack freaks I had to deal with this afternoon sitting around in a circle talking about their feelings. Telling their worst. Hating their fathers. Regretting their mothers. Scared of their camp counselors and Boy Scout leaders.

I can't see how this is helping.

I'm the guy who collects all the trash throughout the day. Three times a day I have to make my rounds throughout the facility. The bathrooms. The gym. The hallways. The cafeteria. The cafeteria is the worst. The food is already garbage when it's cooked, so you can only imagine what it's like when it's thrown away—even if in the trash is where it belongs. At the end of the day, before bed, I have to scrub out the coffee stains and stale pasta sauce and cigarette butts from all the cans.

I sit on the roof all afternoon, overlooking the backyard, the pool—which has been drained. I crawl back in through the window above my bed before the temptation to throw myself off became too grand. I stand outside Timmy's bedroom door for a minute or two, maybe ten. I raise my hand to knock, but think better of it. I head downstairs.

I can't help but wonder how long the folks expect me to stick around. I'm not sure where I'd go, though, if not here. I'm in no hurry to get back to school. I could go to Lynn's, but what would I say to her? The silence that sits between us now, we might as well be on the ocean floor, crushed and depleted.

"Whenever you're ready," Mom kept saying as I unpacked the few shirts I had. She stood in the doorway, not crossing the threshold, smiling amicably and cheering me on from the sidelines even though she knows I'm no good.

She's doing a swell job of making sure this hurts as much as possible. I mean, she took my all my pictures off the walls. I'd hate to ruin my elimination from her life by sticking around too long. When I asked Dad about it on the way up the stairs he said, "We're painting."

Nick calls. He heard I was back in town. He wants to go for a beer. Says he missed me, and damn near wrote me off for disappearing like that.

I wind the phone cord around and around my hand, waiting

for purple fingertips. I ask if we can do coffee instead.

"What? Coffee? You're home for the first time in how long, and you want to go get coffee? You know I don't drink that crap."

Nick says he doesn't like calling the house. What if my parents answer? What would he say to them?

I tell him I haven't had a cell phone since last May.

"How does anyone get a hold of you?"

I agree to go for a beer. This shuts Nick up long enough for me to hang up on him. Mom is in the kitchen cooking dinner. I smell only burnt water and grease. She stands at the stove wearing an awful yellow apron, blinking like she's cutting onions, but she's just stirring water.

She tells me dinner is at seven.

I tell her I'm leaving.

"Where are you going?" she asks.

I'm not sure how much more of this I can take.

I see Dad in the living room on my way out the front door. He's sitting in his favorite recliner. Facing the wall where the television used to be. A cigarette that looks left over and found in his back pocket sits with a slow burn between his yellow fingertips, a paperback—creased and torn—on his lap. I recognize it as a mystery I'd recommended to him ages ago. He's not looking at anything in particular, or maybe, just maybe, he's seeing for the first time in his life.

Seeing what he really has.

I've never seen anything so sad.

Because I see it too.

*

I sip ginger ale mixed with orange juice. Nick orders a bucket of beer. Five bottles for five dollars. It's Thursday afternoon, and the Blue Frog is busier than it ought to be. We have a booth across from the bar. I keep my head down like a local celebrity pretending he'd rather not be bothered for autographs.

Nick asks why I'm wearing sunglasses indoors. "The sun isn't even out today."

I tell him the sun is dying, and pretty soon we'll never need sunglasses again. "I'd like to wear them while they're still in fashion."

Carbonation pops and sizzles behind the bar. Bottle caps dance and clank about in stainless steel sinks.

Nick wants to know where I've been. He keeps slapping the table with both hands proclaiming, "A year, man! A year you've been gone!" Then he starts on a new bottle, and asks more questions before I can provide more answers. Why wasn't I at the funeral? "Your mom would simply burst into tears at the very mention of your name, and your dad, man, your dad just shook his head." This is what he tells me over and over again.

"Tears. Bursting."

He's sorry, by the way, sorry about it all. What a tragedy. That's what he says. He closes his eyes, shakes his head.

Tragedy? He doesn't know the meaning of the word. I want to tell him he hasn't seen anything yet.

Tragedy is compulsive masturbation in all the boys' locker rooms.

Tragedy is an estimated nine hundred sexual partners, and HIV positive at number two hundred and ninety-nine.

Tragedy is this conversation.

"There were rumors," Nick says, "regarding your whereabouts."

Nasty little rumors, I bet.

"Jamie says you found him. She said that's why you weren't there. That it was probably too hard for you." He takes a drink, swallows hard.

Jamie. Always starting something. Leave it to Jamie to find a way to ruin a perfectly good funeral.

"I mean, you weren't at the funeral, man. Right? So, where the hell were you?"

"I know I wasn't at the funeral, Nick. You don't have to remind me every thirty seconds." I swallow the rest of my drink, slamming it down like I want another. Old habits, dying hard.

Nick tells me to take it easy. "Everyone can hear you, man." He runs a hand over the stubble on his head, scratches at his goatee.

"Talk to me about anything but this."

He shrugs. Drinks. "Like what? Like where you've been? Because I don't like the vibes you're sending, man. I can't work with this until I understand what's going on in your head. I mean, a *year*, man!"

I need a cigarette. I have to get out of here.

Nick tells me I shouldn't smoke.

No drinking. No drugs. No sex. I haven't jerked-off in two

hundred and seventy-seven days. I won't even look in the general direction of anything remotely resembling the female anatomy. *I can't smoke?* You'd better have a loaded gun and the guts to pull the goddamn trigger to back up that statement.

"I'll be right back," I tell him.

I slide out of the booth.

There's a girl I recognize from high school at the hostess stand. I can't quite remember her name, but she's got mine down forwards and backwards in case this moment ever happened.

"Nathan Brennan. Hi. Hey. How are you?"

I smile, shrug. I light a cigarette in the foyer.

"I'm so sorry to hear about, well..." she trails off, bats her eyelashes like it helps explain what she's trying to say. "I haven't seen you around lately."

There hasn't been any of me around lately for you to see.

Tess. Her name is Tess. She lost her virginity to Anderson West on the hood of his dad's '67 Corvette during a family barbeque.

Or so the story goes.

She says the barbeque hadn't started yet. "I couldn't make it to the funeral," she says like I was expecting her there and we had to call the whole thing off on account of her absenteeism. I wait for more, a far-fetched explanation perhaps, but she abruptly concludes with, "I'm sorry."

So am I, but not for any reason she'd ever understand.

"You can't smoke in here."

That's what I was hoping.

*

Day 10.

I missed the funeral today.

I was afraid to leave. Afraid I wouldn't return. Showing up, it would have been my funeral too.

Dad came by to tell me Mom wasn't waiting the remaining 20 days. You know what he said to me? "Couldn't this wait?" That's what he said to me.

He lost me as well that day. He doesn't seem to know it yet. Mom does. I hope she'll tell him so I don't have to.

I call Lynn from the payphone outside—the only one left in town.

She doesn't answer.

She never answers numbers she doesn't recognize, and she doesn't answer mine. Not anymore.

There was a letter from her on my desk when I got home. According to the postage, it arrived just days after I left. She didn't have the decency to call, but I wouldn't have called me either.

She kept it short and simple. That's how Lynn does things. No point in wasting any time. She was sorry, sure, but who isn't today? She wrote to tell me she wouldn't be at the funeral. She just couldn't stand the thought of having to see me. Not yet. Not like that. She was the first person I called after the accident. Not my parents. Not the police. Lynn. I called Lynn. Timmy soaked through to the bone in my arms and me crying into the phone, which miraculously still worked after my sudden submerging, screaming everything I'd ever been afraid to say. Lynn picked up because she wasn't paying attention to the caller ID, God bless her heart.

Day 16.

Gary asked me for a light, and asked if I wanted to go to church with him tomorrow.

I wouldn't be surprised to learn that Gary had crawled out of the womb clutching a smoke, asking for a fucking light.

I told him I'd think about it. I'm not sure how church is going to help.

He told me it's not the concept of church I need. It's the people who make up the church.

Half the time I never understand what Gary is talking about, but he says one day I'll get it.

He wanted to know if I'd started talking at group yet.

I haven't spoken a word in two weeks.

Gary said if I want to stay sober, I'd better start talking.

He told me I don't have to stay silent anymore.

He also told me I shouldn't swear so much. I'll never find a nice woman to settle down with, with a mouth like this.

I told him the girls I know like a mouth like this.

He told me I need to meet new girls.

Tess hands me a torn piece of paper with a phone number written in pink. I contemplate taking her into the bathroom and ruining everything I've had going for me over the last year, grounding out what's left of my life in this town with the heel of my boot, but I just smile and take the paper. Her fingers touch my wrist, and I tear her number into a hundred million little pieces before I tell Nick I'm leaving.

I pull the car close to the curb in front of Lynn's parents' house, but she's not there. She's back at school now, up north, studying anthropology and English. My father would be so proud.

Back porches and summer afternoons in the grass, we'd read paperback novels by Kerouac and Salinger aloud to each other, and pray for the days of the beat generation to return. Lynn had this stupid piece of hair that wouldn't stay behind her right ear, and every thirty seconds she'd swipe at it. I've never known anything to be so wonderfully irritating in my life. And in the grass and on the porch, Lynn would hold my hand. And man, she could hold your hand and make you believe, really believe, that there was nothing else in the world but that moment. That hand in yours.

I find Dad in the kitchen. Sitting in the dark of the moonlight. A smoldering ash try and a short glass of half-melted ice in front of him. All this self-inflicted misery is going to put the whole entire family in a premature grave, and for the first time I'm in no mood to die.

"You're home early," Dad says.

I ask what he's doing.

"Thinking."

I take a glass from the cupboard and pour myself some

water. I lean against the sink, and live in the tension because I've got nowhere else to go.

"I blamed you," Dad finally says.

I sip my water.

"But then you came home. And I saw your face. When you were gone, it was so easy to say this was your entire fault. But now you're here. My son. Here in the house you grew up in, and I can't bring myself to hate you the way I did yesterday."

His voice doesn't quiver. His inflections remain monotone. You'd never know the man was crying unless you'd spent eighteen years living with him. Even now it's hard to know for sure. "Now I've got nowhere to dump this but on myself."

I cross my arms and wait.

The upstairs toilet flushes—Mom getting ready for bed.

"When the Hybels next door, when they heard the news, they said to us, 'At least you still have Nathan. Makes us glad we have two kids.'"

I think about slamming my glass against the counter and telling my father to hold that thought while I go next door, and use the broken shards to cut the throats of Mr. and Mrs. Hybel.

"And your mother, she's not exactly handling this well, you know." He pauses, shakes a cigarette from his pack, places it between his lips. The strike of the igniting match illuminates my father's face. I close my eyes so I don't have to see him so clearly. He shakes out the flame.

He offers me one before continuing. I kindly decline.

"She's become a ghost in this house."

"Well, she'll fit right in then."

"She can't blame you," he doesn't skip a beat. "Refuses to. She blames herself for Timmy..." my father says my brother's name like it's the first time it's been spoken aloud since his death. "I found that shit on the computer. When you were in high school. I found the magazines and videos in your room. The condoms in your drawer." I have to grip the edge of the counter while my father speaks these words. "And you know what I said to myself? What I thought? Good for Nathan. He's finally becoming a man."

Then he's crying too hard to understand whatever it is he says next, if he's even saying anything at all.

Day 24.

My name is Nathan Tyler Brennan, and I'm a sex addict. I've been using pornography since I was eleven-years-old. The summer I turned fifteen, I lost my virginity to a high school sophomore I met at Youth Group. I've spent the last five years using up to six hours a day, sometimes more, hardly less, seven days a week. My addiction had me repeat my junior year of high school, destroyed my relationship with the only woman I've ever loved, and because of my addiction, my nine-year-old brother, Timothy Ryan Brennan, is dead.

I drove home to Ohio last April. I hadn't seen my folks since Christmas, and the frequency in which Mom's calls about how much Timmy missed hanging with his older brother increased dramatically enough I had to shut my phone off while the sun was still out.

I hadn't intended to return to Ohio that weekend, but the whole thing with Lynn was still cooling down, and I was tired of sweating it out. Lynn and I had made plans to drive up to Lake Erie for Easter weekend. We rented a jet ski, and bought a new cooler we could pack full of beer and potato chips. It was supposed to be a weekend spent getting drunk on the lake and sun-burnt by the first few rays of the summer sun hot enough to reach us. Instead, two months prior to our weekend plans, Lynn found out she was pregnant. A month later, it was a Thursday, and Lynn slept at my place because she had class a block away from my apartment. It was one of those August nights so thick with heat it smothers your ability to breathe properly. We could taste the mold in every inch of the room. Lost in that state where you can't quite tell if you're dreaming or awake, Lynn had her backside pressed into mine, the friction between us burning our bodies alive. I found my hand between her legs, her arms tangled around my head, me breathing in her endless brown hair that always, always smelled like pineapples and sunscreen.

We faded in and out of that moment, blood rushing to all the wrong places, enabling us to think less and dream more. I woke up later cold and shivering next to her like someone had just spilled a glass of milk in bed. I reached out to find Lynn, to tell her I think something might be wrong, and found her wound tightly in upon herself—knees tucked beneath her chin—trembling and shaking. She pressed her hands to my face, which were cracked and chapped and tasted like copper when she put her thumbs on

21

my lips. I turned on the floor lamp next to the bed, and noticed the crimson color coating the fingers I'd had inside her. I'd never seen so much blood in my life. You'd think a thing like that might bring two people closer together, but in fact it tears them to pieces.

It was Friday night when I got home. My parents were stepping out for their routine weekend date. They immediately canceled the sitter for Timmy, enlisting me for the job. Timmy jumped into my arms. He made me run around the house galloping like a horse. He had two water pistols he kept firing at the cowboys chasing us, and he'd shout, "Faster! They're gaining!" Mom yelled about getting water on the carpet. I came to a sudden stop, bucking Timmy from my back onto the living room sofa where I'd proceed to tickle him until it hurt.

After I got settled in, Timmy asked if we could go swimming.

"Dad just opened the pool!" he squealed. I told him to get a head start. I'd be right out.

"Mom never lets me swim alone."

I messed his overgrown, blonde hair. "You're an adult. Stay in the shallow end. No jumping off the dive until I get out there, okay?"

He took off running to change.

I stopped upstairs to check the email on my laptop. To check Facebook, and hopefully get an idea where Lynn might be. Pictures of her led to pictures of women I didn't know and would never meet. Two hours later my eyes were bloodshot, and I'd made a mess. I glanced up, caught sight of my brother's body floating facedown in the deep end. The computer fell from the bed when I stood. I threw open my window, and slammed into the screen. I punched and tore and kicked my way through, rolling out onto the roof and stumbling towards the edge, the shingles slicing holes in my knees and elbows. My boots caught the gutter and ripped it from the house, and I jumped.

Mom is in Timmy's room. I let the door open without a sound. I watch her sitting on his unmade bed in a long, white nightgown, dust swirling so thick I'm forced to hold my breath to keep from coughing. The place is a tomb. Untouched since last Easter. She's clutching an action figure in each hand—heroes with capes and X-ray vision and gadget belts—stroking their faces with her thumbs.

"Mom," I whisper, I breathe, I cough when the dust collects on my tongue and gathers in my throat.

She looks up at me, lost, like I'm a stranger on the street who has called her name and she swears she recognizes me. Just before I'm about to tell her who I am, she says, "Nathan. What are you doing?"

"I came to say goodnight."

"Oh." She glances down at the toys in her hands. "These belonged to you," she informs me. "Do you remember?"

She holds them up for me to see, and yes, of course I remember. I wouldn't leave the house without them.

"I'm leaving in the morning," I say, and Mom says, "Oh," again.

"I don't know when I'll be back."

"Where will you go?" she asks like it's common courtesy, a

forced conversation with that stranger she swears I am.

I ease myself into the room, like my own mother is a sleeping child I'm afraid to wake. "Mom..."

She smiles, setting the toys on the bed, right where I'm sure she found them.

I get close enough to touch, and stop right there. I kneel before her. "Please, stop this."

She looks confused. Her eyes bloodshot and black like she's been up for days on the worst kind of bender.

"Stop blaming yourself," I take her cold, damp hands into mine, but she doesn't seem to notice. "You're not my mistakes. This is me. All me. Please, let me carry this for you. Please."

She's shaking, the tears escaping in short bursts she can't keep down, and I've got her frail frame scooped up into my arms as she slides from the bed. Somewhere within all that pain I can hear my name, over and over again, escaping her lungs.

"I love you. And I'm sorry," I say, my hand on the back of her head, her face buried in my shoulder.

"I'm so sorry. I'm so sorry."

Day 31.

I've decided to drive across the country.

Gary wanted to know why. Was I looking for something? And why wasn't I going home?

I told him I want to see the world. I'm not ready to go home. He wanted to know if I wasn't ready to face myself.

Maybe he's right. I don't even know who I am without the sex, the pornography. Then he said to me, nothing but the butt of the cigarette between his chapped lips: Just make sure while you're driving, you're looking here.

He poked my chest with a wrinkly, yellow finger.

He said something like: People are always looking everywhere but where they came from.

I have no idea what that was supposed mean. I feel like we spend our whole lives trying to escape where we came from.

He said it's okay, and that all I need to know is that he loves me know matter what.

Can you believe that? He loves me for me.

We hugged for an uncomfortable duration of time by my standards, but I let it slide.

Stay in the tension, Gary said to me. Learn to live there.

He broke the hug first, and told me to get my ass to a church.

I take my father up on his offer, and share a smoke with him on the back porch. The laughter of children playing tag fills the night air. It's colder than it ought to be in May. I tilt my head back, releasing smoke rings into the black above us. It's hard to imagine flaming masses of light tearing through the universe continuously exploding and expanding, so massive they dwarf the sun, when all these stars look so peaceful from here.

"Where have you been?" Dad asks, his voice sounding the way it does when someone speaks to you in a dream.

"I went to say goodnight to Mom."

I pick tobacco from my teeth.

A dog barks.

"I mean since you left rehab." He doesn't look at me when he speaks.

Crickets sing songs only they can understand.

"I drove across the country. Twice."

"By yourself?"

"Yes."

Silence, true silence, is a father dragging on a smoke at nine p.m. on a cool spring night with one dead son, and the son responsible for such a tragedy sitting next to him.

Tires screech. Cars with the windows down and the music too loud drive by.

After an eternity I hear, "Your mother was worried sick about you."

"Sure."

"I knew you were okay." He reaches out, puts a hand on my shoulder and squeezes. Never once have I ever heard my father say he's proud of me, or say that he loves me. After tonight, here in this moment, I won't be left wondering.

He releases the pressure on my shoulder, and I miss him already. "Did you find what you were looking for?"

He stubs out his cigarette on the concrete steps, grinding it to ash and filter. My lighter in hand, I release the flame, holding it out until it burns my thumb because this is a moment I do not fear. I want to remember this moment forever.

"No," I tell him before we're doused in darkness, again. "That's why I came home. I was looking for me."

MIRACLE

NOW: THE EIGHTH OR NINTH OF DECEMBER

Eve is in complete hysteria. Clutching her stomach, arms a tangled mess around her abdomen. She's on her knees spewing Spanish, and in all this madness appears to be smiling. Her husband, Edwin, if I'm not mistaken—we've yet to formally exchange pleasantries—holds her; rocks her as though she's a feverish child.

Things didn't quite work out the way we'd planned, did they?

I need to call you because this is the end.

I need to tell you I'm sorry.

I'm so damn sorry.

Edwin gets a good look at me, but he's keeping distance. He shouts, "She's saying it's a miracle. That you're a miracle!"

Grateful for Edwin's translation of his wife's wet gasps of exclamation, I don't quite think either of them is thinking clearly because she couldn't possibly have said this is a miracle. Eve is traumatized. Obviously. And Edwin's delusional. The cut on his forehead won't stop bleeding. Plus, he's wearing only one shoe. I don't trust a man who wears only one shoe. I would hardly begin to describe this scene as a miracle. I've never been the type of guy to believe in a thing like that. Things like miracles.

I've got a mother who insists on them. Three years before my miraculous conception, a tumor was removed from her ovaries and the ability to reproduce life went right along with it. "How could I not believe in miracles?" she's always saying. "I've got you for a son." Not only that, but she also believes God has a plan for my life—I'm destined for something huge, right in Ohio. "Why else would He have chosen me, of all people, to bring you into this world?" Mom still says.

The joke's on God, though, because I left Ohio the day I turned eighteen and never looked back. I didn't accomplish a thing while I was there except graduate high school, and give Emily Thompson her first orgasm.

Edwin is still shouting. He's making a scene. People love a good scene. "It is a miracle. You are sent from God!"

The Greyhound parked on the eastbound side of the highway, all its passengers are making their way over—a field of cell phones and camera flashes floating ominously like some out-of-this-world entity.

Six or seven days ago, three thousand miles of unforgiving highway, and a desolate heart kept us apart. Yet here I am. My triumphant return to the Midwest. Who says we can't go home again?

The cold concrete beneath me is beginning to become uncomfortable. I shift my weight. I smile and nod in annoyance at Edwin when he tells me to stay still.

Help is on the way, but I am helpless.

I used to think a miracle was just one of those things you've got to see to believe. However, in this particular case, it takes being part of a miracle to believe in one. You could call it being in the wrong place at the wrong time if you want. I'm certain everyone else will simply describe this as an act of heroism because they'd have to know how this story began to call it anything else.

But maybe that's the business of miracles.

Which is a shame because 'tis the season.

SIX OR SEVEN DAYS AGO

The phone rings.

Light pours through the window. My soul scatters like the cockroach it is for the nearest shadow. I twist and contort beneath my only set of sheets. My skin breathes fire. I've slept in my clothes again.

Ring.

I catch sight of the sun adrift in a liquid blue sky.

I wish it would rain.

Ring.

The constant stream of exhaust and strained engines passing by the window tells me it's early. Everyone else in Los Angeles has somewhere more important to be today than here.

Ring.

My throat itches. My shoulders ache. I swallowed too much regret last night. My stomach is in no mood to negotiate this morning.

The machine clicks on.

Leave a message. No promises.

"I wish you'd change your number and not tell me," is all you say. Not exactly euphony. There's a breath. Then a dial tone.

The machine clicks off.

You must have needed someone to hate today.

It'll pass.

After vomiting in the bathroom, I run cold water through my hair. I clean the sleep out of my eyes, drinking corroded city water from the cup I use to hold my toothbrush.

A loud thud and crash originating from the apartment next to mine shakes the entire bedroom. I hear muffled shouting; a few words that could be considered offensive if you happen to be on the receiving end of them.

I pull my face away from a dirty bath towel, and stagger into the kitchen. Pouring orange juice over ice, I mix in vodka so it goes down easy. The fresh liquor sterilizes my stale morning breath.

Tired of that flashing red light, I rip the cord from the wall and drop the machine in the trash, breaking glass. After two years of this sort of insidious behavior, you'd think one of us would've developed the guts to do the right thing. Or at least fight back.

The beat-up hardwood floors are cold this morning against my feet. I wish I had a pair of slippers. I rub at a deep scratch on the wood with my big toe as though it were a scuffmark easily removed. The previous occupants of the apartment had an enormous dog responsible for my distressed floors. I can still smell its wet breath when it rains.

I make my slow way downstairs to the small café directly below the apartment.

At this time of morning, this time of year, the sun is useless. I bury my hands in my pockets, bunching my shoulders to my chin to keep out the cold. Cars speed east and west on Fountain Avenue. Judging by traffic, it's maybe eight-thirty. Time stands still under my roof because I am out of batteries, and the day doesn't seem like such a waste when there is nothing to count it down.

Feeling content I have nowhere to go and couldn't conform if I wanted to, I slip into the café. The smooth aroma of fresh ground beans and hot water warms me inside and out. The only stragglers here are the usual out-of-work locals and artists from the neighborhood. Danielle is working. She always greets me with a smile that's a bit too loud.

I ask for a large coffee. She fills a cup from a thermos labeled: *Breakfast Blend*. I drink it black. It's too strong. It always is. Danielle doesn't charge me. She wants to know what I'm doing later. I pretend to care about an abandoned newspaper on a table to my left.

"You should come over," she says.

At that I look up. Danielle fiddles with the large, black bracelets and rubber bands she wears to conceal the vertical scars crawling about her wrists. We sleep together on rainy days and starless nights, but it's nothing more than an attempt to forget bad memories. Her black hair hangs loose and tangled around her neck like it hasn't been washed in days. She tells me she's cooking dinner. She always makes too much and would hate for it to go to waste. Danielle knows I lost my job. I can't tell if this is sympathy or something more.

My stomach rumbles at the thought of dinner, sloshing around this morning's cocktail.

The mailbox is jam-packed with useless ads and irritating bills. A week's worth of unchecked deliveries tumbles out. I sift through the mail on the floor with the toe of my boot: Two credit card statements, a letter from the insurance company, a cell phone bill, a letter from the cell phone company. I pick that up. Read it. Return it to the floor. The type of white paper envelope concealing birthday cards and other congratulatory nonsense catches my eye. A Christmas card from Mom. Full of cash. Full of guilt. A message that reads: *I hope this helps*. Red lipstick smeared where she kissed the card. There's not enough here for a plane ticket, but there's certainly enough to get me drunk this afternoon. It's nice to have a mother unintentionally looking out for your worst interests. I drop the hundred bucks in my wallet, and leave the card with the ads and other junk mail in their rightful place on the ground.

*

A door slams upon my arrival to the second floor. A man maybe four inches shorter than me, but built like a Grizzly Bear with a growth defect, pounds his massive fists against a door he's been put on the less fortunate side of. He must feel someone watching him. He takes a break from all his cursing and pounding to inspect me like I might be a better snack.

I drop my head; fiddle with the mail and keys.

I slip inside my apartment uneaten, just in time to hear my neighbor declare he will be getting the shotgun from the truck. I open a closet in the small foyer, and take out a wooden bat my grandfather carved as a child. I sling it over my shoulder and step back out into the hall, but the bear is gone.

I shower and change into a pair of jeans I've avoided sleeping in this week. I'd like to bring a bottle of wine to Danielle's place. I grab a jacket from the closet to fight off California's December. The hallway is empty and lifeless. All the ads I left in the foyer downstairs are stacked in a neat, square pile at my feet. Soft, orange light snakes its way out from the crack beneath Ray's door across the hall. The light shifts, and I know the son-of-a-bitch is watching me through the peephole. I kick his precious stack of ads into a flurry of paper snow, giving him the finger on my way out at no extra cost.

I've got your number punched into my cell. The letter in the mailbox from the phone company informed me I've got roughly forty-eight hours left to use the thing. Forty-eight chances to call you back.

I push END, and return the phone to my pocket.

Forty-seven.

The wooden floors inside the Hole on Fairfax look wet with stale beer stains and stomach bile. The tables all appear to have been stolen from junkyards and trailer parks; rusty legs and green plastic tops cracked and peeling. A jukebox croons country, and a black velvet pool table looks to be the local hangout for a gang of Greasers.

On any given day, The Hole is the perfect place to find the scum of the earth before noon. However, despite the name, Saturday afternoon attracts a rather pretentious crowd of washed-up industry professionals and waiters pretending to be actors. I take a seat at the bar, really feeling the cold, hard stool through my jeans. It's the only empty seat left at the counter. I'm caught between a two-hundred-year-old woman mining through her purse for one more quarter so the touch-screen poker machine at the counter will keep dealing Blackjack, and a beautiful redhead with skin so pale it illuminates this cavernous tavern.

I don't even speak and the bartender sets a dirty glass of pale, amber liquid in front of me. I nod and try to smile my thanks, but he's already gone about his business. Two stools down, next to the redhead on my left, a regular cowboy chewing toothpicks between chapped lips tells a joke about three monkeys pushing a wheelbarrow full of salt into a bar.

The cowboy's surrounding audience of drunken spectators laughs at their best attempt to slip back into minding their own business. The bartender grunts or coughs or giggles, and the cowboy, he says to the redhead: "What's your name, sugar?" The word *sugar* comes out the way any alcoholic who's missing a few teeth and had trouble with the letter S growing up would say *sugar*.

I can't be sure if I'm drinking beer or water from the tap that the bartender pissed in to give it color. Whatever the case, I ask for another.

The redhead, she tells the cowboy her name is Angel.

"Well that just confirms my suspicions," the cowboy slurs, sipping his beer.

"And what suspicions are those?" Angel's voice is soft with a bit of Nashville country lurking around the vowels.

"That you fell right outta heaven." I can smell the cowboy's words from here. They stink of chilidogs and Budweiser and cliché.

"Hmm. That's cuter than you know." Angel swivels in her stool to face me, placing an elbow on the bar and her head in her hand—shooting me a lopsided smile and perfect teeth. "Hi. Want to buy me a drink?"

I think of you. I think of Danielle. I shrug and say, "Sure."

It's noon. College football spills across the television screens.

Angel orders a shot of Tequila with a Corona to chase, and that's half my tab. I'm almost mad about it.

She asks if I live around here.

I tell her I do.

She smiles, and wants to know why I look so sad, but I could swear I'm smiling. "If you want to talk about it," she says, "sometimes strangers make the best listeners."

The bartender delivers our drinks. He has the hairiest arms I have ever seen. If I ran into him outside of here, I'm quite certain I would mistake him for a Sasquatch.

"Why's that?" I ask.

"Why's what?"

"Why do strangers make the best listeners?"

"Because they're never really listening, just waiting for their turn to talk." Angel slams her shot. I try to keep up. Everything burns going down, and when I come around, ready to ask if Angel wants to get out of here, an underwear model with hair I'm sure always looks that good and liquor running through his veins comes between us. He tells Angel they got a table in the back. She's gone with a wink and smile, and I fucking hate L.A.

"Tough day, huh?" The cowboy wipes his nose with black, greasy fingers. "Name's Cleatus, but call me Cleat. All my friends do." Cleatus holds out his right hand, his left tugging at the brim of a ten-gallon hat. I force a smile. We shake.

The Sasquatch slides Cleatus another round of water and piss, sets another full one in front of me.

Cleatus picks up his glass with unexpected daintiness. He sips. He licks his lips and sighs. Tells the Sasquatch he'd like his check. He's driving across the country and doesn't want to stop every twelve minutes to drain the pipe. "If you know what I mean." He smiles at me. "I mean take a leak." He laughs, nudges me with an elbow. "Jesus, partner, lighten up. It's game day."

I'm unreasonably hostile.

Angel sits on the underwear model's lap. Four other men at the table act as an entourage making obscene gestures at the screen. Or at the girl. Maybe the guy she's with is famous or something. It's hard to tell. Angel tries to run her hand through the model's hair, but he smacks her away. She appears undaunted. My heart hurts.

I think Cleatus says, "It's a damn shame, a pretty little thing like that…"

I take out my phone to check the time. Two missed calls.

An 800 number and you. No voicemail.

I look at Cleatus. He's eating toothpicks like pretzels. I ask, "How far across the country you going, Cleatus?"

He dutifully reminds me all his friends call him Cleat. Then he's all too eager to tell me he's going home to the woman he lost. "Tell her what she deserves to hear. Why, you lookin' for a ride, partner?"

Cleat's Ts sound like Ds.

The underwear model slides his hand up Angel's skirt. She swats him away, but he doesn't relent. I hear, "bitch," I hear, "slut," or maybe I'm just making up excuses to get back in God's good grace. I no longer need one when Angel's face meets the rough wooden walls of this establishment.

I'm relatively certain Heaven has already locked me out and

revoked my weekend pass, but I still look for every excuse I can to get God's attention.

I'm off my stool and across the room so fast by the time I reach Angel's table, I'm not sure if I walked or wished myself here. My memory is half obliterated by the Tequila.

She's got her face in her hands. No one seems to be paying her much attention. It's as if she doesn't even exist. I'm suddenly second-guessing myself, wondering if I am seeing things. I should have eaten breakfast this morning. "Excuse me."

I've got the guts to fix everything with everyone but you.

The occupants of this particular table are so transfixed on the television I almost believe the game is the only thing happening on the planet at this very moment.

I look at my hands. I'm still holding my half-full beer mug. I've spilled a bit on my jeans.

"Excuse me," I try again. "I'd like to have a word with the lady in the booth."

The underwear model finally takes his attention away from the television above his head. He inspects me from head to toe, and when he no longer considers me a threat to his survival in the food chain, he wants to know what the hell I am talking about.

I sigh, point at Angel. "A word. With her. Please."

The men turn their attention to the corner of the booth, amazed, it seems, that there appears to be a woman amongst them.

"Do you know where you are?" the model asks, not as if I've simply misplaced myself and walked onto the wrong side of the high school cafeteria, but as if I quite literally might be insane. I check my outfit to ensure that I am not wearing hospital whites.

His entourage laughs, and one of them tells me I'd better get while the going is still good.

I can take a hint, but I'm dying to feeling something. Anything.

I slam my glass down on the table. The entire thing shatters upon impact, leaving me with nothing but half a handle and a hand full of beer-soaked shards. It's just as well. The whole act was solely intended to be more of a display of my masculinity. Still, it would have been nice to have a bit of something to defend myself if things don't go my way.

The bar falls silent except for the hundred thousand screaming fans at the Bowl Game. The Sasquatch cranes his stubby neck in my direction. It won't be long until he breaks up all the commotion.

The underwear model doesn't even ask to turn at a dozen paces and duel like any proper gentleman should. He just swings, slamming his iron first into my jaw. I'm not sure if the next one comes from him or his entourage, but I'm suddenly blind in my right eye.

Our spectators cheer respectively, or maybe it's still the fans at the game. The Sasquatch attacks. He drags me, shoves, me, downright degrading me across the entire length of the bar before opening the door to the outside world, tossing me onto the pavement. I land next to a puddle of vomit, smacking my swollen face against concrete, and it's a blackout.

*

A MEMORY OF US

The hardened blanket of snow on the ground muted the world of both color and sound. A sputter from the car's exhaust disrupted the ill-fated tranquility.

The car seat was freezing. I spent the better part of an hour scraping ice off the windshield, and the heat still hadn't kicked in. I moved my hands in and out of fists to keep the circulation moving.

I was already thirty minutes late. I promised I'd be there early.

We were scheduled for the first appointment in the morning.

You said it was a sign.

You said we were doing the right thing.

You said you loved me.

I said nothing at all.

Inside the apartment, I found you tongue-tied; balled up on the floor of the bedroom, a trail of tissues—your breadcrumbs—leading the way. Looking up from a photograph, you told me I was late.

Cold Chinese take-out sat uneaten on the coffee table. The apartment reeked of it.

"I had to dig the car out," I said taking off gloves, wiping my running nose with the back of my hand. "Of all nights to get hit with a snow storm...Jesus."

You blew your nose into an already-used tissue. Your over-sized, red and blue ski jacket swishing and cracking. You tightened the scarf around your neck, pulled the matching hat down around your ears. "You'd think this was one thing you could have been on time for."

"Stop it." The sharpness of my words cut through that room made of ice. I took a breath; counted to ten, spoke quietly.

The words "stop it," echoed off the walls.

In that jacket, you were a turtle hiding in its shell.

"I'm just tired. I'm working full time here." I said. "I've got this covered."

"You're such an idiot. Stop acting like this makes you some sort of hero or something."

"A hero? Like I'm proud to be doing this? I'm doing it for *you*."

"You're doing this for you because you can't stand the thought of living without me, you selfish prick."

"Come on," I said, our silence striking fear in the most unbreakable of hearts. "We're going to be late."

"We're already late."

I offered you my hand, and you took it. But it was no comfort to either of us.

In the car you told me you were sorry. Your words came out in whispers, buried beneath the snow.

"I know," I said. "Me too."

You wouldn't let me come inside. You left without a word, and left me there alone. I drove around in circles for twenty minutes, suddenly hoping they hadn't called your name.

I parked the car in a *Loading Zone Only,* running the three blocks to the clinic, slipping on ice, bounding through sidewalks that hadn't been shoveled. I called out: "Stop!" and "Wait!" and "Don't do it!" which was silly because you couldn't hear me. "I love you! Do you hear me? I love you!"

More nonsense.

I shoved my way through pro-life protesters, through the front doors, and into the waiting room. You were nowhere. I asked the receptionist if you'd signed in already. She said yes. You had. The procedure was already under way. I'd just have to wait.

Out of breath and my lungs pierced with icicles, I took a seat.

I dropped my head into my hands, begging for forgiveness for the life we'd just taken.

I'd never felt so alone.

THE SECOND OF DECEMBER. OR THIRD.

Cleatus wants to take me to the hospital.

I try telling him it's just a scratch.

"They knocked your head about pretty good in there. And that bartender, he was havin' none of it."

"Really, Cleatus, thank you. But I'm fine." My world is a sickening blur of dark gray matter. I pull the visor down. I have to wipe away a layer of dust and dirt to find the hidden reflective surface I'm looking for. The left side of my face has ruptured into an unrecognizable mass of swollen skin and blood.

"You can call me Cleat, you know. All my friends do."

Oh. Right. I forgot.

I have an uncontrollable desire for French Fries. It's dark outside. I don't see a clock on the dash. I'm trying to figure out how I ended up in Cleat's car to begin with.

I shut the visor.

"Are you sure I can't ride you to the hospital?"

I wiggle around in my seat. Everything rattles. Either the noise is all in my head, or this vehicle is being held together by nothing except a couple of loose screws. "I need a drink, Cleat."

"I don't think that's such a good idea in your condition."

"Nonsense. I drink to keep myself in this condition."

We're riding in a pickup. There's no back seat to inspect. The floor beneath me seems rather sparse of anything to drink, but I can't be certain of this observation. My feet appear to be settled atop six dead rabbits, hard as stone, and I don't really feel like digging around beneath them.

"Taxidermy's kind of a hobby of mine," Cleat says. "Sorry about the inconvenience. They don't mind. You can leave your feet there."

I mind. I lift my knees to the dash. My feet dangle. Twelve black marble eyes all staring up at me.

"Where are we going?" I ask.

"I figured the hospital, but you keep on tellin' me otherwise."

"Oh. Right. The hospital. No hospital. Just take me home."

"Where is home?"

I consider the ramifications that may develop from a guy named Cleat driving a pickup full of dead, stuffed rabbits knowing my address.

Cleat tugs at the brim of his hat, looks at me without easing up on the gas, and I'm wondering how he's able to drive so fast in the gridlock-riddled city of Los Angeles.

"Wait. Cleat. Where are we?"

TWO, MAYBE THREE DAYS LATER

The sun seems to be of a bit more use out here in New Mexico.

I stumble out of my motel room looking for the Laundromat I saw when I arrived last night. I was able to open my right eye this morning—the swelling having gone down significantly—but it still hurts like hell to squint.

Yesterday over breakfast, Cleat told me he was driving across the country in search of the woman who broke his heart. He shoveled globs of pancakes soaked with maple syrup into his mouth. I choked on dry toast and black coffee, doing my best to care. He said that's why he thinks we should stick together. Against my better judgment, I guess I told him how much I missed you. He said he wanted to help us reunite.

"Partners in crime," he said.

I tried to tell him I should call you first, but we all know how well that's been going.

Cleat swallowed and said, "When you didn't want to go to the hospital, I wasn't sure what to do with you. Then I thought, well, I could use the company, you know?"

No. I didn't know.

"We're like Butch and Sundance." His teeth cracked through burnt bacon. Little black bits stayed stuck and left behind when he smiled.

I wondered if this whole thing qualified as a kidnapping. Would anyone even pay for my ransom? Mom, maybe. I thought about asking Cleat for the keys to the truck. We'd be Thelma and Louise, and I'd drive us right off a fucking cliff.

"This girl," he said after rinsing out his mouth with a glass of warm milk. "My girl, she left me for another man. Now they're having a baby. Should have been mine."

I tried picturing a second Cleat walking around the planet, and decided one was enough. "Maybe it's for the best."

"For the best?" Cleat put his fork down. "The guy's some illegal immigrant and *she's* gonna runaway with *him*? *And* have a child? I'll be damned. I'll be Goddamned. If I can't have a baby with her, no one can." Cleat then picked up his fork and continued eating pulpy, dissolving heaps of pancake.

I tried to keep my toast down.

Cleat held out his fork to me with what looked like already-chewed food speared to the end of it. "You wanna bite?"

After I kindly declined Cleat's offer for a "bite," and later refused to assist him in the bloodbath I imagined would be the reunion with his beloved, he decided we couldn't be partners anymore. "You understand, son. I've got to leave you out here. You tell anyone where I'm going, and I'll kill you dead. You understand."

Now I'm stranded in this desert with nowhere to turn but towards you.

I start walking.

*

I make change at a twenty-four hour laundry service twenty yards down the road from the motel. Outside, darkness falls fast. I drop quarters into a payphone tagged with bumper stickers and graffiti. I close my eyes, my thoughts surfing the dial tone. I already know how this conversation's going to go.

On the fourth ring you'll answer groggy with the sound of sleep, the unawareness of where you really are. It'll take me ten minutes just to tell you who's calling.

You'll tell me the time like I don't know, and ask what I am doing.

Returning your call. Well, calls.

After an excruciating duration of intentional silence, you will do me the courtesy of asking how things are. Just a formality.

I will ask about you, and you'll tell me you're still alive. Or maybe you'll tell me you miss me.

The pit in my stomach will swallow me whole.

I want to tell you that I am sorry, and will you ever forgive me. But I won't. I will tell you instead I loved you both, and I should have said it that day.

But you'll stay strong, saying you'd have done it anyway, with or without me.

I will say you don't mean that. I abandoned you, and I couldn't even look myself in the eyes for what I'd done, so how could I expect you would have any less trouble looking at me? I let you end our child's life because I loved you. The pressure it would have put on your heart, you'd have died in the delivery room. And

46

it would have been my fault.

Can't you see? Don't you understand? I did it because I didn't think I could live without you.

When I tell you that I've finally decided to come home, you will say something like, "You don't have a home here anymore." And even though you always said words could never hurt, I'll take off my shirt and show you all the scars that surround my heart just to prove you wrong.

The dial tone cuts off. I slam the phone back on the receiver. The quarters spit themselves out.

A rusty pickup with one headlight crawls down the desert road like a wounded coyote. I think of Cleat. I wait until the taillights are nothing more than two red eyes staring back at me in the distance before I make my presence known.

There's a repairman in the Laundromat seemingly fixing dryers. He's on his hands and knees when I approach him, a can of beer on the floor to his left. He's chewing black tar and biting dirty fingernails as he stands and introduces himself as Isaiah. He agrees to let me hitch a ride with him to the bus station. He kicks over the can of beer. It's empty. He finishes the terms of our agreement with, "As long as the next six pack is on you."

I only half-listen to Isaiah. I'm high off the fumes of paint thinner and gasoline mysteriously coming from nowhere inside his van.

He's curious to know if I'm on the run from the law. Not that it's any of his business, he's sure to reiterate.

"I almost wish I were. It'd make more sense."

"More sense?"

"I'm trying to tell someone I'm sorry."

"Well, what are you waiting for?"

"The nerve to do the right thing."

Isaiah cracks open a beer behind the wheel, offers me a sip. I gladly accept and drink half the can. I hand it back, and he shakes his head, already opening another. He offers to buy my bus ticket back to you after I explain what we'd done.

"Why do you want to do that?"

He tells me to simply pay it forward.

"Like the movie?"

"Like the movie. I'll be damned if that little boy isn't a fine actor. Wouldn't you say?" He sips his beer.

"Yeah. Sure. He's great."

"Damn fine acting."

Isaiah stares off into a starry desert night, probably watching the movie all over again in his head.

I'm on the edge of sleep, and Isaiah asks, "Do you promise?"

Sick and disillusioned, I suddenly remember where I am and what's happening. "Promise? Promise what?" I guess I fell asleep. My neck has become a wooden plank. I can't feel my right arm.

"To pay it forward."

Massaging my neck, shaking out the sleep in my bones, I inform Isaiah that life is not a movie.

I promise him nothing.

"That's okay," Isaiah says with his hand on my shoulder. "You will." I shrug him off. I close my eyes. He asks where I'm going.

"Ohio. Akron, Ohio."

"You're a long way out from Ohio here."

"Yeah, well…"

"You want to tell me more about it?"

I've told him enough. "No. Not really."

"Okay. Well. If it helps change your mind at all, sometimes strangers make the best listeners."

TWENTY-FOUR HOURS LATER

Five hours from you in Cincinnati, a bad corndog gets the bus driver sick. It's two a.m. at a rundown rest stop on an unseasonably warm winter's night in Ohio. Most of the passengers take this opportunity to get off the bus, stretch their legs, and clog up the facilities. The toilet on the bus has been out of order since yesterday.

I pace around the parking lot. I check the payphone with the severed cord over and over again like it's going to fix itself when I'm not looking.

The roads are empty tonight, uncommon for this time of year. Hands in my pockets, I slip away from the crowd, wandering across the highway to the rest stop on the westbound side. I'm hoping for a phone in working order.

The parking lot has been abandoned. Only a lonely pickup remains. I hesitate, but when I catch sight of a man taking a nap, his head resting against the passenger-side window, my heart eases up on the gas.

The payphone next to the men's room appears to be in working order, but who am I kidding? You won't believe me until I'm on your doorstep, and even then you might doubt yourself.

I drop the phone back on the receiver. I'm all action and no talk.

Over here the smell beginning to emanate from my clothes and skin is more noticeable.

I step into the restroom. The fluorescents flicker in sync with the dripping faucets, my heels clicking against a tiled floor wet with piss and overflowing toilet water. Mirrors cracked and caked with layers of hairspray and body fluid. Made-up languages and graffiti lettering scribbled in black marker paint the stall doors; the last one on the left opened. Uninviting shadows sob quietly in the corner.

"Hello?" I whisper.

The quiet cries fall short. Then silence.

I make my way closer. "Hello? Are you okay?"

Nothing but the *drip, drip, drip* of faucets.

Tucked away inside the last stall I find a woman, frail and caving in upon herself. She's balled-up in a puddle of what could be water, inserted between the wall and toilet. She's got her knees pulled under her chin. Black, frayed hair hangs loose in all directions, hiding her face. I rap my knuckles against the open stall. Her neck snaps back to get a good look at me, her eyes expecting someone else; her feet trying to gain traction against the wet floor.

"Whoa, whoa. I'm not here to hurt you." I reach my arms out

because it feels like the right thing to do, but she won't let me get anywhere near her. I ask if she's hurt because I don't know what else to ask. Her nose is bleeding. Her face swollen. "I'm going to go get help, okay? There's a bus full of people on the opposite side of the highway. I will be right back." I speak slow and careful like she might be the dumbest person on earth. Her eyes beg me not to leave.

"No?"

She starts firing off words in Spanish.

"Whoa, hey, it's okay. English? Do you speak English?"

"Don't leave me," she gasps like forming those three words is the hardest thing she's had to do all year.

"There's a bunch of people right across..."

"Please."

"Come with me," I whisper. "It's okay."

She keeps her knees under her chin, chattering teeth, arms wrapped around her shins.

I step into the stall. There's not enough room here for the two of us. The stall door is all bent out of shape as though it's been kicked in by someone who didn't have the time to be civil about using the toilet. I have to shut it to fit inside. I kneel down, careful to stay balanced on my feet. I don't want to be kneeling in whatever is on the floor. "What happened?"

She starts speaking Spanish. I don't know why I asked. Or what the hell I am doing in here. I talk over her. "Let me get help. Come with me." I need to get out of here. I'll miss the bus.

"What if he comes back?" she whispers.

"If who comes back?"

"My husband."

"Your husband did this to you?" I slide a bit close, reaching my arm out like she's a stray dog I'm trying to pet. She shudders, shaking her head. "No, no. *Where* is my husband? Where?"

"Your husband? I don't know. I haven't seen anyone else. There was a pickup…"

Her eyes go wide.

"Eve! You still here, baby?"

I've got this poor woman wrapped up in my arms, my lips to her ear whispering, "Shh, it's okay. I'm not going to let him hurt you," but her vibrating body pulsates against mine with such ferocity, I'm sure it can be heard.

"You didn't run away did you, Eve?" His words are thick and full of isolation.

Footsteps come to a halt at our stall. "Eve."

This woman wrapped up in my arms, her heart is going to beat itself right out of her chest. My back is to the door, holding her tight.

"I love you, Eve. I'm doing this for us."

Click.

The shot is loud enough within these four walls I barely hear the succession of the following rounds. The force of the first bullet ripping through the stall door sends it flying open, smacking my back. The swinging door apparently assaults our assailant's aim because the second bullet brings down tile from the back wall, white dust and porcelain falling around us. The third bullet collapses the toilet tank; a breaking dam and we are swept up in its current. We slip and collapse. Eve on top of me. Me looking up at Cleat standing over us, tugging the brim of his ten-gallon hat, a look of shock on his face. A six-shooter in hand.

"Cleat?" my voice scratches. I taste blood.

"Partner?"

The blur of a man high on vengeance crashes into Cleat, smashing him into the wall on my right. Eve starts screaming, burying herself into my chest. This sends an unrelenting amount of pain through my spine, into my brain. The lights above my head flash hot and white before turning to black.

The *drip, drip, drip* of the faucets.

"Who are you?"

My eyes flicker and fight the light above me.

"Answer me!"

On my back, soaked through to the bone.

"Tell me who you are! What were you doing here?"

I strain my neck. A dark figure stands above. I am staring down the even darker barrel of a gun.

Shouting in Spanish, I only catch, "There are people. People on their way over!"

Is that a threat? I can't tell if that's a threat.

"Answer me!"

I can't feel my legs. I want to get up, but I can't feel my legs.

"Please. Don't hurt him!"

I get my head off the floor, using my elbows for support. I'm underneath a row of sinks. A milky trail of red runs from the bottom of my feet to the last stall on the left. Cleat lies slumped over and lifeless against the wall.

The man with the gun, he's got it right in my face. He's hopped up on adrenaline and misinformation, telling me I had better answer him. He says he's going to pull the trigger. This guy, he's wearing only one shoe. There's a hole in his white sock. His big toe pokes through.

The woman I found in the bathroom stall, the woman I believe to be Eve, she's at this guy's feet clutching and clawing his ankles, saying: "He saved my life! He saved my life!" Then she goes on and on again in Spanish.

"Who are you?" I ask.

"Is this true?" the man wants to know.

"I...I don't...I don't know." My breathing is shallow, labored.

"She says you found her in the stall."

Eve, she starts up again with all the Spanish. "Edwin, Edwin," is all I can catch.

Edwin drops the gun. A switch apparently flips in his brain. He goes to the floor with his wife. They hold each other through all the commotion my organs are making during their last plea for life. "I need help,"

Edwin looks from his wife to me with eyes that seem to be seeing me for the first time. He pries himself away from his beloved, and slides to my side. "You've been shot," he says.

Oh, you are never going to believe this.

"A phone," I say. "I need a phone."

Edwin nods. He keeps nodding while patting down his pockets.

"I call the ambulance."

"Get me out of this bathroom."

Edwin keeps nodding. He gets a good grip on my arms, careful not to get anywhere near my wound.

I take one last look at Cleat then do my best effort to help Edwin. I grab at the edge of a sink, finding the strength to pull myself from the floor. I stumble out of the bathroom, into the night with Edwin, dropping back to my knees. I clutch my stomach, feeling around for something that shouldn't be there.

There is no exit wound.

Edwin screams for help, waving his arms like he's been lost at sea for ten years and the Greyhound bus across the highway is his rescue plane. He turns to look at me, at his frantic wife on the ground. "Help is on the way. They will help you."

I slump back against the wall. I hold out my hand. "Phone. Please."

Edwin feels around in his pockets. Then he says this is a miracle. He tells me Eve says I am a miracle.

I shake my head. Edwin hands me his phone. "Thank you." I can't remember your goddamn number. Please. My thumb strokes the keypad, feeling for a memory.

When it finally comes, my hands are shaking so badly I have to dial three separate times before I get it right.

The phone to my ear, the line connects, begins to ring.

"It is a miracle. You are sent from God!" Edwin shouts.

"God sent you to be here! Right here!"

Ring.

"I'm no miracle, Edwin."

Ring.

"No," Edwin says. "Not Edwin. Adam. My name is Adam."

Adam. Right. Sorry.

Ring.

"And it is a miracle," Adam or Edwin says. Whatever. "If you weren't here, my child would have perished along with my wife."

"Your child?"

Ring.

"Yes!" Adam exclaims, still clutching Eve. He kisses her face. He wipes her bloody nose. "My wife is pregnant. She's four months pregnant!" He kisses her stomach.

Ring.

My life fades to black.

Ring.

The credits begin to roll.

Ring.

Ring.

You answer, your voice groggy with the sound of sleep.

"Hello?"

WE CAN'T GO HOME AGAIN

The phone rings.

I ask Sarah if she minds. She wrinkles her forehead, upset that I would still think to ask such a thing.

I answer. Hello, Jane.

My sister speaks, "Dad's dead," and something inside me collapses. All the faulty wiring and veins tangled around my heart are yanked from deep within like ripping plugs from an unsuspecting outlet. I fold the newspaper I am reading into thirds so my hands have something constructive to do.

Sarah cries for me.

You don't have to be on the phone with Jane to hear her through the receiver.

Fernando, the guy behind the counter, he refills my coffee. Tells me someone was in here earlier looking for me. "He was wearing a suit."

The look on Sarah's face says this really isn't the time.

I shrug. The place is empty.

I ask Fernando if he got a name.

"Are you in trouble with the police?"

I want to know if Fernando asked for ID.

"No, but he was in a suit, you know? So I just figured."

I take the Red Eye back to Ohio. It's raining when I arrive.

The day they brought me home from the hospital, he spray-painted my name against the backboard of the basketball hoop in the driveway.

A tornado in June ripped it into oblivion.

Mom hugs me at the front door. She wants to know why I wasted my money on a rental car. The scar down her left cheek makes my face itch.

The house smells of burnt coffee and over-stayed welcomes.

There's a photograph around here somewhere with his arm around me. We're both wearing silly hats. I'm sure it's in a box or at the bottom of a drawer.

I spend an hour in the dark on the basement steps trying to remember what it was like sitting here at seven-years-old eating dinner alone because I talked back at the table. Somehow all this dark is scarier now than it ever was before.

It rains for the funeral. There's a tingling sensation beneath the skin on my face where he hit me the first time. Someone puts an umbrella over my head and the feeling's gone.

It's always fucking raining here.

Jane is conveniently missing from the day's festivities.

"Quite the turnout," Mom says leaning into me.

He knew a lot of people.

"But did any of them really know *him*?"

A woman I don't recognize cries and shakes, holding herself because no one else seems to want the job. At least someone here has the dignity to show a little respect.

He danced in our living room with my date to the Prom, and I didn't know how to tell him to stop.

Sarah calls. Tells me someone came by her apartment. Some guy in a suit. Looking for me. "What kind of trouble are you in?"

I tell her not to worry. I'll be back tomorrow. But lock the doors and check the windows. Maybe she should stay with her brother.

"Do you want to talk about it?" Mom asks.

I stare at the tree I fell from when I was ten and broke my leg. He told me to get up, stop crying, and cut the grass. I haven't cried since.

I tell Mom there's nothing left to talk about.

I find Jane at home in the front yard with her son. The rain has stopped, and he's stomping on earthworms.

"You've grown up," she says.

At least one of us had the guts to do it.

"Someone came by here earlier today looking for you. He was wearing a suit. I thought he was part of the precession or something. Turned out he wanted to know if you were in town."

I bailed him out, I tell her. Paid his debts. Dad came to me in tears, looking for help. Jane doesn't believe this. The part about the tears. I don't blame her. I was never very good at lying. Anyway, it's me they're after now. That, at least, is the truth.

Jane wants to know how I could be so stupid.

I tell her it's hard not to love your father.

She asks where I am staying. I tell her at a motel.

"You can't go home again," she says. She smiles. She puts her hands on her hips like she always does when she knows she's right.

My nephew, all smiles, stomps the life out of a big, juicy one.

Jane invites me inside for dinner.

A car pulls into the driveway. The crying woman from the funeral steps out, an old shoebox tucked beneath her arm. Crows feet scratch at her eyes. She looks uncomfortable in those heels.

"Dad's girlfriend," Jane says to me, but I wasn't asking.

"I wanted to give you this at the funeral," the supposed girlfriend says. Her voice makes me desperate for a glass of water. "But it was raining and I feared it might get damaged. It's all he owned in the world. He would look through this box every night before bed."

I take the box because Jane has turned away, her attention redirected at my nephew and the massacre he's heading up in the driveway. The girlfriend steps back as though she's passed along the torch, her duty done. She gets back in the car without a word.

I remove the lid on the box. It's filled with old photographs of us. Jane. Me. Dad. Laughing. Smiling. In love. I dig through memories long forgotten, a sadness welling up inside in which I have no control—broken pipes spewing water. On the backside of a particular photo—Jane sporting a cowboy hat and boots to match at the age of ten—Dad wrote in his jagged, crippled handwriting: *Janey. My everything.*

Jane is still crying in my arms when the rain starts again.

I never got to tell him I forgave him, and he never once said he was sorry.

But I'll be dammed. He loved us.

MORNING DOESN'T COME

She slides into the booth like she's fallen from the sky, dropping in from thirty-seven thousand feet just to ask why she's been dragged here so early in the morning. The duct tape holding the torn, red vinyl seats together groans and stretches against the sudden onslaught of her heroin-thin frame. She wears flip-flops, and stubs her toe against the door on the way in. It's all she can think about.

The sunglasses she wears are too big for her face, and he's glad to see her take them off.

His face full of stubble, he knows she won't want to kiss him goodbye.

He's already ordered their coffee.

She sips and complains that it's cold, and he says, well, they were supposed to meet at seven.

"I know, why so early? Where were you this morning?" She tucks her feet beneath her legs, her toe throbbing all the while

"Can you believe how hot it is already?" She's looking out the window like you can actually see the living, breathing entity the summer heat has become.

"I'm going away," he tells her, getting right to it. No sense in wasting any time.

The air is thick with bacon grease and burnt coffee. They'll smell it all the way home until they finally get a shower, and into a fresh change of clothes.

"Really?" She wants to know where.

Her pale, blue eyes are gray today.

"I can't tell you." His hair is getting long, but not long enough to keep it tucked and secured behind his ears. This frustrates her.

"I'm not sure I understand. Why can't you tell me?"

"Because I don't know where I'm going." He keeps biting his thumbnail, wishing he had remembered to clip it this morning.

"You don't know?" She can't help but think this all seems a bit over-dramatic.

"No."

It's too loud in here for her. All these early-morning commuters turning their newspapers page-by-page, talking on phones clipped to their ears. She enjoys her coffee at quiet cafés, and her breakfast in bed. She says pancakes taste better that way.

She asks him, "Then why would you leave?"

"I have to get away from this place."

"What?" They've been in *this place* their whole lives. Why on earth would he want to leave? Their friends are here. Their family.

The waitress walks passed. He motions with his empty mug

for more coffee. "You're no good for me." He says this like he's talking about saturated fats and not the woman he's been sleeping with for two years.

"What do you mean? I thought we had a good thing going here."

"I've never even been to Pittsburgh."

She sighs with relief. "Is that where you're going? It's not that impressive there."

"I'm just saying. I've never been *anywhere*. And there's got to be more out there than...*this*."

"When will you be back?"

"Maybe tomorrow. Maybe never."

Quite skeptical of his declarations she says, "You don't know where you're going and you may never return?"

"That sounds about right."

She wants to know if he's taking anything with him.

"I put some clothes and an extra pair of shoes in a bag this morning. It's in my trunk."

"You packed before you left?"

"Just the essentials," he tells her.

"Your toothbrush was still on the sink when I got up."

"I can buy a new one."

"You know I hate waking up alone."

"And to think how much we used to hate going to bed alone. We just can't win."

She's had enough at this point. His elusive statements. The cold coffee. The early morning. "Why don't you tell me what's really going on?" She wants to know so she can go home. Back to bed where she'll enjoy a proper breakfast.

"Do you have any hobbies?"

"What? Hobbies?"

"Aspirations? Dreams?"

"I think I am going to get promoted to assistant manager before the holidays."

The waitress refills their mugs. His mug. Hers is still full of coffee and getting colder.

"That's it?"

She laughs. What more could there be? "That's good money, you know."

She knows he's not exactly making good money. Maybe that's what this is about. Some sort of masculinity issue.

"I like to write," he says. "Did you know that?"

"I know. I found your suicide notes."

"Don't take it personally. It was just something to pass the time."

She sighs relief. "I get it."

"I hope so."

"This is all metaphorically speaking."

"This is me getting behind the wheel and putting as much distance between us as possible without driving into the Atlantic."

Her feet are falling asleep. She can no longer feel her toe. This pleases her. "Are you going away because you plan to kill yourself?"

He picks up the dinner knife, twirls the tip of the blade

against the table.

"What will I tell my friends?" she asks.

"You never tell them anything. I can't imagine there being an issue."

She wants to know what he'll do for money. Did he quit his job?

He tells her he simply isn't going in today. "They'll figure it out."

"Don't I get a say in this?"

He's being unfair. He says so. "I guess that's being unfair." Then he says, "Go ahead and say what you'd like."

"I'd like you to stay."

"Is that all?"

She shrugs. "More or less."

"Let's talk about less."

"I feel like you've just brought me here to prove something." She sips her coffee and makes a face like she's surprised it's cold. "What am I supposed to do without you?"

"All this time, you've only wanted me the way you wanted me." He pauses. "For the first time in my life, I'm finally ready to be me." He returns the knife to where he found it. "I have to go." He takes one last sip of coffee knowing it'll only be a matter of minutes before he'll have to stop somewhere and use the bathroom.

"Now?"

"It's all I've got." He stands.

Looking up at him she wonders aloud, "Can't this wait until

tomorrow morning?" She's confident this will pass.

"And if morning doesn't come?" He plays with the change in his pockets.

"Morning always comes, silly."

He looks out the door to a world he's all too unfamiliar with.

Looking back at her he says, "That's what scares me."

He leaves enough money on the table to cover the bill.

She touches her toes to make sure they're still there.

"Goodbye, Tomorrow." He walks away.

She orders the pancakes. They just don't taste the same.

HIGHWAY MILES

We'd been living together, the four of us—me, Roger, Chad, Jade—for six months when we met the writer.

Roger had been squatting in a house along with Jackie and Daphnee outside of Jacksonville on four acres of land I'm not sure the government knows exists. Jacksonville is a real shit city. Everything out there looks whitewashed, and takes on the unflattering characteristic of appearing to be melting in the heat. The closest neighborhood to the house is half a mile away and full of middle-aged black men riding around all day on rusted bicycles, and old women wearing sweatshirts in August who always feed the stray cats.

Jackie claimed it was an old fort—a hideout, or something—that used to belong to the naval base near Jacksonville Beach. She knew about the place because supposedly her grandfather crashed there during the war.

"There are tunnels running for miles under the house," she

would tell us.

Tunnels extending all the way to the coast. You could access them from the basement. We took her word for it because no one ever wanted to go down there.

Not after what happened to Roger.

When you asked Jackie, "What war?" she'd get this look in her eye like you might be plotting against her. She'd tell you we've been at war since the dawn of man, and we keep renaming something that's never ended.

This is not a fun conversation to have with Jackie.

Roger went down there once. Down to the basement. Right when he first started squatting with Jackie and Daphnee. He attested to Jackie's story about the tunnels. He told us about a crawlspace behind a small, wooden door, which seemed to lead down to the darkest, coldest parts of the earth.

Roger was down there for seventeen minutes. When he finally came up, he started sleeping on the second floor balcony and didn't speak for nine days. A tuft of hair on the right side of his head had turned white.

We used the house in Jacksonville when we had nowhere else to go. None of us had a permanent address. Roger was the only one who could stand living with Jackie and Daphnee for more than a week. He stayed behind more often than not. Even after the incident in the basement.

Jackie and Daphnee weren't terrible people or anything. They were just in love, and the whole world falls away when you're in love. Or something like that. Doesn't mean you stop buying toilet paper. They never attempted to make the house hospitable after they took up residence there. They were eighteen at the time, dropped out of high school, and ran away from home. Anyway, they found the house, this haunted hellhole, and remained off the grid ever since. The faucets pumped out brown water, and the roof leaked whenever it rained. And it rains every day in Jacksonville.

Are they still at the house? You mean, Jackie and Daphnee? I don't know. No one does. We came back one day, and they were gone. Just gone. Roger thinks it was the house. He'll tell you they must have gotten high one afternoon, wandered into the basement, and the house just swallowed them up.

Either way, before they disappeared, their door was always open, and it's nice to have a place of familiarity to return to every now and again. Even with that mysterious basement.

Not that I believe in ghosts.

We tried to get the writer to go down there when we first met him.

"Why does Roger still live here if something so traumatizing happened to him?" the writer asked, chewing on a pen cap, but not the pen.

"Because the rent is free, and heroin ain't cheap," Jade said, sitting on the counter, painting her toenails purple.

*

How did we all meet? Living on the road is just like living in any other town anywhere else in America. You frequent the same bar enough and you're bound to run into someone you know, someone you hate, and someone you could love.

The writer told us he stayed with a family of artists in Philadelphia during the coldest month of the year. "Their house," he said, "was too old and too tall to heat properly."

He said he spent most of his days huddled on the stairs to the third floor, the only spot in the house that heated evenly.

"And there was a wolf," he said. "In the house."

Taxidermy.

I'd been on the road for over two years. I'd never seen a wolf, and I didn't miss home.

"They ran a skull cleaning business out of the basement." The writer referred to his notes to be sure he was relaying the details accurately; always flipping through that notebook.

If you're going to be accurate with the details, I don't understand the point of being a writer.

"Nine people lived there. The walls of this house literally vibrated with their creativity. The whole place was alive and breathing," the writer said, which is such a writer thing to say. "That's why the wolf bothered me so much. It was the only thing in the house that didn't move."

"Jade was bit by a wolf once," Roger informed us. It was one of the rare occasions Roger actually joined us on the road. He'd spend weeks at a time in his room. I thought the sunlight would do him some good. So we sat in a field somewhere off I-10 headed west.

"It was a dog, not a wolf." Jade rarely speaks above a whisper. She had her head in my lap, so I might have been the only one who heard her. I was watching Chad's hands. The way he handled her bare feet. Jade's skin is so pale I swear to God a hug can mark her forever. I wanted to tell Chad to be careful, to watch what he was doing.

Jade smiled. It was so bright outside, she had her eyes closed and still needed to squint. She was the only one of us not wearing sunglasses. Jade never wears sunglasses. She says the sun provides some sort of vitamin for our eyes. If she's right, Jade will have the vision of a bat, and we'll all be blind and helpless by the time we're forty.

I told her this once. She responded by telling me that when she has a daughter, she hopes her little girl has the same fiery red hair she does. Jade doesn't think her hair will be so vibrant by the time she's forty. I'm not sure what it had to do with blindness, but sometimes I think Jade is the only one of us who truly thinks about the future. A future where there is still hope for us.

"What are you doing on the road?" Chad asked the writer when they met.

"He's a writer." Daphnee had this habit of answering for other people. I never minded because I tend to think more than talk.

The writer nodded.

"Can't you do that sort of thing from home?" Chad asked.

"The kind of writing I do, I can do it from anywhere." Flipping through his notes, he said he was on a spiritual journey.

"You trying to find yourself or something?" Chad drank beer from a glass jar. Jackie and Daphnee only had glass jars to drink from. "The road is the best place to do it. You'd just better find it while there's still time."

The writer showed up looking for a place to crash. He'd answered an ad Daphnee posted on Craigslist down at the Jacksonville Library. They needed the money and figured some sap looking for a roof would pay them.

They kept a revolver under the pillow, so there was nothing to lose, really.

The writer showed up while we were all congregated in the living room, passing around jars of beer before sleeping through the weekend.

"Still time?" the writer asked.

Chad believes we are on the brink of the Apocalypse, which means we believe it too. Well, maybe not Jackie and Daphnee. And you'd assume Jade could think for herself, but spend enough time with Chad, and you'll forget you ever had the luxury. Chad went on about his conspiracy theories regarding aliens and September 11th; about China and all the billion dollar ghost cities they're building. And, of course, America will end up rebelling against the government or a Chinese invasion. Whichever comes first. He says we will take to the streets. Naturally, they'll be looking for a leader. That's where Chad comes in.

Roger asked the writer if he was a journalist.

"No, I'm not a journalist."

"Who gives a shit if he's a journalist?"

"I thought you said you were a writer?"

"You look like a cop. I think he's a cop. Are you a fucking cop?" Sometimes I think Chad believes he's living in a Tarantino movie.

I tell the writer if he sticks around long enough, we'll give him something to write about. Then I mentioned the basement.

"Chad," Jade called from the kitchen. "Who gives a shit if he's a cop?" She emerged in the doorway like a ghost. In all our time together, I never saw her in anything but those cowboy boots with the soles peeling off and cutoff shorts with the pockets hanging out. She was a walking magazine ad for the post-apocalyptic generation we were all counting on. She cut out the necks out of all her black t-shirts so everything she wore hung off her deteriorating shoulders. It was obvious she never wore a bra. Her red hair raged like fire against all that black.

Everyone listened when Jade had something to say.

The writer, if he was sweating us, he never showed it. "I think cops have bigger things to worry about than a couple of punks who don't pay taxes or rent because they think the world is ending."

A blade in Chad's hand, he said, "That sounds like a very 'cop thing' to say, if you ask me."

Sometimes I wished the movie *Reservoir Dogs* had never

been made.

Chad and Jade? I don't think they'll ever settle down. Wherever they are. They'd burn suburbia to the ground if they stuck around too long. I mean, there are kids in suburbia. Gardens. And little white dogs.

The writer wanted to know what it is we did for a living. He was chewing that pen cap, looking for a blank page.

"We don't do. We live." I thought that was good, and hoped the writer put it in his little notebook.

"Okay, so how do you live? How do you earn money?"

"Panhandling. We dive in dumpsters for food. We show up at the front doors of extended family when we need a good meal. And when we have the extra cash, we treat ourselves." I acknowledged the all-night diner we were sitting in at two a.m. and sipped my coffee. I didn't tell him about the times we siphoned gas in truck stop parking lots, or when Chad stole the revolver from Jackie and Daphnee to knock over a liquor store because he was bored.

Not that I thought the writer was a cop, or anything.

The writer was tired. He drank coffee all day long, which I think made it worse for him.

The writer said something about Jade. How Jade doesn't seem like the type of woman to eat out of a dumpster.

"Jade," I told him, "...Jade isn't the type of woman to eat out of a dumpster. Because Jade never has any trouble getting what she wants."

If it wasn't for Jade, we'd all be dead by now. Or working nine to five behind a desk somewhere. Which is practically the same thing.

"I'm still not exactly clear on what it is you guys do, though."

I asked the writer how he made money while traveling. And if he's paying rent back home. And where home is.

"Home is in L.A.," he said. "And I'm not paying rent. I gave up my apartment so I could travel as long as possible."

The bells on the door crashed against the glass. Chad stumbled in. The diner was void of customers except for us, and the waitress who chewed her gum like she was devouring her own tongue. Chad immediately spotted us.

"And the money?" I asked the writer.

"I guess you could say I live off the kindness of strangers."

"And when you hit the road?"

"What about it?"

"What did that feel like?"

The writer spit a piece of black plastic from his mouth.

"Freedom. Like I'd been a prisoner my whole life, and now the world was mine."

"The whole world *is* yours. Is that the secret to happiness?" Chad asked like he'd been a part of the conversation all along. He dropped himself into the booth next to the writer. The table settings clattered.

He smelled detestably of sweat. Even through all the bacon grease and burnt coffee in the air.

I asked where Jade was.

"Sleeping in the car."

"Freedom isn't happiness," the writer answered. "We're all free. But true freedom is being able to have whatever you want and being okay without it."

Chad smiled and slipped one of the butter knives off the table and into his pockets.

I wanted to ask him if he'd be okay without that goddamn notebook.

At one of those traveling centers dropped in the middle of nowhere, USA, I caught a trucker squatting down on the backside of his vehicle to get a good look at Jade as she rummaged through the trunk of our car. I turned to look at the writer. He saw it too. His hands twitching like he wanted to do something.

Like he wanted to protect Jade. Only Jade never needed protection. No one ever cared to admit it, but she was the one protecting all of us. She kept the whole operation together.

"Hey!"

Chad emerged from the gas station, a coffee in each hand. I turned back to the trucker in just enough time to see him struggle to stand up-right, his enlarged gut disrupted his center of gravity as he waddled over to the cab for safety.

Chad set the coffees on the roof the car. Jade shut the trunk and asked, "What's wrong?"

"Hey!" Chad called again, ignoring her. Or maybe he just never heard her. "What the hell are you looking at?"

The trucker and all three of his chins shouted back through the gap between the cab and the haul, "Mind your own goddamn business!"

"That's exactly what I'd like to talk to you about," and without missing a beat, "Jade, baby, open the trunk again for me."

Jade opened the trunk. The driver told Chad to watch his mouth.

The writer swears he heard the driver say, "Watch your fucking mouth around a pretty little thing like that," but who can trust a writer? Anyway, if he had said a thing like that, well, I'm glad Chad didn't hear him.

A tire iron in his hand, casually hanging at his side like a regular gunslinger, Chad made his move.

The driver, even though he weighed twice as much, was smart enough to recognize a man like Chad when he saw him. A man like Chad, he actually goes through with using a thing like a tire iron when he has one.

The driver clamored back up in the cab by the time Chad reached him. I told the writer to get in the car. Jade was already sitting shotgun like she'd seen this episode a thousand times before.

The writer asked, "What about Chad?" like they'd been best friends all along.

I wasn't a baby sitter. Not for Chad. And certainly not for any writers still wet behind the ears. I got in the car hoping he would understand he was on his own if he stood there for another twelve seconds.

He clamored into the backseat by the time I had the key in the ignition. The sound of shattering glass, and I threw the vehicle into reverse.

"He just broke the guy's window!" the writer's excitement made the whole scene more thrilling than it actually was.

Jade had her feet against the dashboard, painting her nails ambulance red.

I swung the car around to the truck, and told the writer to move over. Chad jumped inside like we did this sort of thing all the time.

"Can you believe that guy?"

I put the car into drive.

A cup of coffee exploded against the back windshield.

Chad and Jade? They weren't together. No. At least not by society's definition of the word. They were together more by the definition that if Chad found out Jade and I have been sleeping together, he'd castrate me. Not because they appeared to be in a committed relationship. But because we were committed to Chad.

This is how we spent the majority of our evenings: sleeping on the walkways of billboards towering above the highway.

Up there you start to think you just might not live forever.

The highway endless and rushing by beneath you.

The writer was taking notes. I knew this because his responses slowed up, trying to absorb everything. He'd left his notebook behind in the car.

I had a tape recorder waiting for him in my glove box. I just wanted to make sure he appreciated it before I gave it to him.

"Where do you think they're all going?" Jade asked. She loved that game. She was sitting on the edge, dangling her legs above the traffic. Fearless.

I often wondered when we were up there, if the passengers in the cars believed we are part of the billboard. Part of the advertisement of the American Dream.

"Home to their beautiful houses and five car garages. Home to their debt just to get a few minutes of sleep before waking up to go to work to try to pay it all off again. It's all worthless. Slaves to themselves and to a collapsing government."

"You know," the writer spoke up, "not everyone is as rich and spoiled as you think they are. Is this why you guys do what you do? Because you think you are better than everyone else?"

"You think people here are rich?" Chad scoffed. "We've all lived beyond our means. It's only a matter of time before this country gets taken over or blown to hell by North Korea. The world is coming to an end, man. You know it just like I do. You're just like us. And that's why we are on the road. It's the safest place to be when everything starts to fail. We will be the ones people look to for answers. We will know all the places to hide. We will know how to defend ourselves. We will be kings. And the road will be our Kingdom."

Up there it was perfect chaos.

"Are you really living then?" the writer asked.

The writer wasn't looking when Chad pulled out the

revolver, and thank God because I think he would have had fallen right onto the highway below us if he'd turned around. And I don't know which would have been worse: watching him splatter below, or watching a bullet remove the side of his face above. He'd been sitting next to Jade, dangling his legs over the edge right along with her. I leaned against the advertisement for Bunker and Bunker Family Law. Chad stepped toward the writer, his arm and the gun filling the remaining distance between them.

"I don't think we know what it's like to be alive until we've died." Chad was channeling Tyler Durden, and I wanted to speak up, to say something, but I knew the gun was loaded, and it would take me weeks to fall asleep without thinking of the writer with no head. "Until we've lost everything."

I could tell Jade knew what was happening, but she didn't even flinch. She just smiled and winked at the writer with her one eye that wasn't black and bruised, her red lipstick providing enough light in the night for us to see.

"Which is what you've done?" the writer asked, his eyes seemingly focused on the traffic below, on Jade's toes dangling near his. "You've lost everything?"

"Which means we now deserve everything. And while the world is panicking under the chaos of it's destruction, we'll be living just fine. "

"So what are you doing now then?"

Chad adjusted his grip on the gun. "What am I doing now?" He looked at me like I was supposed to tell him. Like he needed me to make sure he was, in fact, still holding the gun to the writer's head.

"Exactly. What are you doing now? Are you truly living, or just killing time?"

When the writer finally turned around to smile, to face the destiny he didn't know was waiting right behind him, Chad had already tucked the gun into the back of his pants.

The writer had been with us for almost a month when we finally returned to the house in Jacksonville. The windows were nailed shut, and the front door had been replaced with plywood. Chad stood in the overgrown, yellow grass smoking cigarettes. The marsh was closer to the front steps than I remembered. I imagined an alligator stalking Chad from behind.

"What do you think happened to them?" the writer asked. He'd found the note from Roger saying the girls were gone, swallowed by the house, and he was moving west. I've actually seen Roger twice since then. They weren't chance encounters. I'd heard he was in rehab, and went to visit.

The writer sat down next to me on the front steps. I think he stepped in alligator shit because the wind carried a foul smell of rotting garbage and human waste with it. I scraped the soles of my shoes against the wooden steps.

I shrugged. "Maybe they finally realized nothing lasts forever."

"Good for them," said the writer. "Good for them."

The sky was thick and gray, consuming the horizon.

I told the writer it was going to storm just to have something to say. I didn't say much else, though, in case the house was listening.

Jade stood to our left, at the corner of the wrap-around porch. The wind whipped her hair across her face. She looked out into the wasteland sprawling before us.

Or she was nowhere near us.

I hoped Chad's cigarette would start a fire.

We ended up in a motel that night. The writer recommended we keep moving because of the tornado warnings, but Chad insisted we stop. We could only afford one room with two beds. There were four of us. The writer was the first to suggest he would sleep in the car. Which seemed ridiculous to me since he was the one who showed concern for the tornados in the first place.

Three men and Jade in a motel room with only two beds.

"Jade and I will take this bed." Chad sat on the edge, unlaced his boots. "Sleep in the car if you don't want to sleep next to your friend there."

Jade said nothing. She went to the bathroom, locking the door.

The writer's arm brushed against mine. I put a little distance between us. Chad lay back on the bed, a cigarette between his lips in a nonsmoking room.

The last of the day's sunlight cut between the curtains, making the place look black and white and suitable for Humphrey Bogart or Frank Sinatra. I thought of Jade's skin, and the bruises around her thighs that weren't there two days ago. "You don't own her," I heard myself saying, immediately hoping no one had been listening.

Chad blew smoke, but kept the cigarette pressed between his lips. He tucked his hands behind his head. "Jade's our only hope for the human race. Especially now that the lesbians are gone. Not that they gave us much hope to begin with." Even in the diminishing light, I could still make out all the yellow beneath the arms of his white t-shirt. "I found you. I took you in. I've let you tag along on every adventure, every ride, and I've never once complained, never once have I given you shit. I let you have a roof over your head..."

"Jackie and Daphnee let me have a roof over my head..."

Chad opened his eyes, removed his hands from behind his head, and sat up. He took the revolver from the back of his pants, and set it on the nightstand. Heavy metal clunking against wood, and the whole room felt colder. The cigarette hadn't left Chad's lips since he lit it.

"If you don't like it here, you are welcome to leave whenever you please."

The writer asked for the keys.

Chad stood. "They're in Jade's purse." He shoved his shoulder into mine on the way by even though there was more than enough room between us. He traveled with a wake of second-hand smoke. "Don't drive away in the middle of the night," he said, and opened the door. Light spilled in, then it was black again.

The writer and I sat on the curb outside of the motel room

drinking coffee and smoking cigarettes. Since meeting the writer, coffee is all I drink anymore.

"Why do you let Chad make all the decisions?" he asked.

Because the woman he thinks he controls is sleeping with me.

"Because every group needs a leader."

"This entire country is yours. You could go anywhere you wanted. Yet you're here, at a motel in Missouri with a man who thinks he's going to be king of a fallen world, a writer, and a woman who seems to be along for the ride until the next one shows up."

I wanted to tell him not to talk about Jade that way. She'd never leave us. She'd never leave me. "So what about you then?"

"I left home because I didn't know the world existed beyond the box I'd contained myself in. It's easy to forget God could exist when you start forgetting there's someone else out there other than yourself."

"There is no God. You'll see soon enough."

I'll never know how long Chad had been standing there, but when we turned to look, his back was to us and he was already closing the door to our room.

"What do you think happened to Jackie and Daphnee?"

I told the writer I still didn't believe in ghosts.

"I hope it was ghosts," said the writer. "But I also want them to be okay." He took a sip of coffee. Mine had already grown cold. "You think you're living in freedom here, but you're afraid to leave. You're all slaves the same as the rest of the world you're trying to set free."

Back in the hotel room, we found Jade sitting peacefully among the debris of misplaced anger. I couldn't tell where the blood on her face originated from, or if it even belonged to her.

She twirled a piece of broken glass in her hands.

Chad sat on the edge of the bed closest to the door. His back was to us. The gun hung peacefully between his legs, the barrel threatening only carpet.

The writer said something about calling the police, and before I could tell him not to, he started to run.

The gun fell from Chad's hand, and thumped against the floor. It wasn't as menacing as a gunshot, but I jumped anyway. He turned to look at me. His face was paler than usual. The beard he had grown no longer made him look rugged and confident. Suddenly he was no better than the homeless men wandering the streets of Los Angeles.

I stepped forward. Only because the gun was on the floor and I loved Jade.

Chad dug into his pockets, pulled out a cigarette.

I hesitated between Chad and Jade. I kicked the gun under the bed, and carefully navigated what was once a fancy looking vase, many of the shards the same shade of red as Chad's hands.

Jade sat on the floor in her underwear, and I feared what the back of her thighs were going to look like when she stood. "I'm sorry," she spoke in her quiet voice.

I knelt down beside her. "What for?"

She twirled in her hands, not glass, but the knife Chad had pocketed at the diner all those nights before.

The writer appeared at the door. Silhouetted against the parking lot nightlights he looked like he was in the business of abduction and zipping around the galaxy. The only comfort he gave me was the pen and the notebook I could still make out in his hands.

"For what I've done."

"What did you do?"

Chad's lighter clicked. Nicotine and tar filled the room.

"Where will you go?" her voice grew quieter. I still couldn't figure out where all the blood properly belonged.

"Go?"

"I've assassinated your leader."

The writer's silhouette disappeared from the doorway, letting the streetlights make their way back in. We didn't see him again until the sun came up.

The police never showed. And in the morning, Chad was gone.

It was just the writer, Jade, and I after that. The sky above us turned as black as the pavement we drove on, and I couldn't see where the road ended and the clouds began.

The radio turned to static, and the writer kept telling us to pull over under this bridge, or that bridge over there.

The low fuel light had been on for days.

The roads were empty. I could smell the rain, and feel the

electricity in the air.

I remember desperately wanting to turn to Jade, to ask her if it was the ending we'd heard so much about. Had Chad been right all along? But I needed to keep my cool. I needed Jade to know I could function just fine without Chad.

The sky met the pavement a hundred yards in front of us, and I brought the car to a stop so we could watch as God dragged his fingers across the earth.

The writer was, surprisingly enough after all his concern about the bridges, the first to get out of the car.

Jade quickly followed.

I looked out through the back windshield. We were alone. Not a house, not a car, not Chad, not even a cow. Nothing but us and God.

It was our time.

What I thought was a stone struck the car. Or maybe it was a golf ball picked up and thrown by the wind.

The writer and Jade stood in the center of the road, holding hands like they were awaiting judgment. Waiting to be set free. All I held on to was the steering wheel.

I got out of the car, only to be struck in the shoulder with a piece of ice the size of a softball. It knocked me to the ground, taking the wind right out of me.

"Jade!"

She turned at the sound of my voice, the electricity in the air had all her hair standing upright.

"Get back in the car!" I shouted.

I could see Jade's pale skin glowing in the lightening, her body already bruised from the hail we couldn't escape. As she and the writer returned to me, I ushered them into the car and sealed us inside.

I pushed Jade down in the front seat. The windshield started to crack beneath the onslaught of hail and debris. I covered her body with mine.

I recall the writer shouting something about the sunroof. The only reason I believe this is because moments later the sunroof shattered. Glass and hail rained into the car, pummeling my back and head.

I couldn't tell if it was Jade shouting or me.

The frame of the car twisted and bent. I couldn't help but think I'd put us inside a trash compactor for safety.

It was like one hundred helicopters in the sky, descending upon us.

And then it stopped.

Just like that.

Silence.

We emerged from the car as though we were the last three people left alive. For all we knew, in that moment, we were. The hail was already melting beneath our feet. Jade informed me my forehead was bleeding; her red hair all out of place, and I'd lost count of the bruises on her arms.

The writer's face was full of tiny flecks of glass, but he was smiling. Smiling in a way I'd never seen anyone smile before.

The sun blasted through the blanket of clouds above us. Jade put her arm around me. It was so hot outside the pavement became soaked in steam as the water evaporated.

The writer, he was holding his notebook—at least what was left of it. The pages were torn, and the cover missing. On the remaining pages, the ink ran blue and bled. He flipped through and laughed. He finally took that pen out from behind his ear, and he threw it. The notebook followed close behind. He put his head back and his arms out as one does when they want to catch a snowflake on their tongue.

He started shouting.

Jade moved closer to me.

The writer started dancing.

Jade kissed my neck.

The writer smiled and screamed the way God probably intended babies to smile when they entered the world before sin got in the way: happy to have arrived, and excited to start living.

THINGS JUST FALL APART

Purple hair knotted through purple fingers, James rinsed his hands in cold water.

Purple lips and that sick, sinking feeling.

He kept his hands under the faucet until he couldn't feel them anymore. Until they were purple too.

Reflected seventy-seven different ways, they'd made a mess and he was getting dangerously used to it. He flipped the bathroom light off, watching his step for deadly traps set by broken shards of misused glass.

I want to sleep for days, he thought, *wake up and laugh at how young and stupid we used to be.*

He crawled onto the bed, staying above of the covers. He could smell her. He was going to be sick.

He dropped to his knees on the bathroom floor without any respect for the mirror and all its new locations. Tiny flecks of glass lodged themselves into his skin, or pulverized completely between his knees and the floor.

He missed the toilet.

He didn't care.

He'd clean it in the morning.

Stella was due to be discharged from the hospital at nine a.m. James waited in the lot out front. He was using a rental car. The least he could do was offer Stella a ride. Maybe they could go to breakfast. He considered flowers, but he didn't know her all that well. What if she was allergic? She might not even like flowers. He wouldn't be surprised if she was the kind of girl who didn't like flowers.

Stella wore glasses and jeans, a t-shirt, and Converse. A plastic grocery bag swayed at her hips containing the clothes she'd been wearing when she arrived. The nursing staff suggested throwing them away, but she was rather partial to the black and purple blouse in question. They washed it for her instead, cleaned it as best they could, but their best wasn't enough to get it all the way new again.

An unlit cigarette clung to her bottom lip.

She limped just slightly so that you'd miss it if you weren't looking for a girl with an ankle full of pins and screws. She commented that her neck still hurt. Those gorgeous green eyes of hers were tired and defeated. The stitches intertwining through her right cheek were scheduled to be removed the following week. James tried not to look at them. She might be self-conscious.

She said they itched.

He'd never seen anything so beautiful in his life.

Stella patted down her pockets. It was something to do—looking for something she was well aware she didn't have. She asked him for matches.

James didn't carry matches. He didn't smoke. He offered to take her to breakfast. She said he didn't have to, that he'd already done enough. She didn't have any money anyway. An insurmountable amount of bills weren't going to disappear overnight, but he insisted. His treat.

She was just trying to be nice. The truth was, after a week's worth of hospital food, she could've killed for greasy, burnt bacon and runny eggs that didn't taste like the plastic they were served on.

James painted. Stella performed.

She had a gig in two weeks and invited him when she declined his offer to visit the modern art museum that Saturday. Some of his work was on exhibition. A promotion for emerging young artists.

She hated his music. He didn't know any of hers.

He liked to read. She liked to write.

He was nice. And he was there for her now. But Stella wondered if he was coming on too strong. This *was* a little weird, wasn't it? Especially after the accident. They talked about it. James did most of the talking. He knew the details. How could he be so forgiving when she couldn't even forgive herself?

She asked about his head, if everything was okay.

He took the week off from work to rest. He was supposed to get the results from the MRI back any day now, but the doctors said he probably had nothing to worry about.

She danced, and mentioned to him that they might go to the club after the show.

James was all left feet and elbows, and politely said no.

He loved her hair. She loved his smile. "I like your teeth," Stella whispered, coquettishly biting her bottom lip. She played with her spoon, twirling it around the edge of her mug.

His leg jack-hammered dodgy and fast beneath the table. The silverware rattled. He hoped she didn't notice. She barely moved since they'd sat down.

He made her laugh. She made him think.

He regretted his tattoos, and she wanted more.

"I'm sorry," she said. "I really screwed up."

"It's okay," he told her. "I forgive you."

"My lawyer said the court would give me a sponsor. Mandatory meetings."

"It's not as bad as it sounds. Trust me."

"Thank you," she said. "For not pressing charges. You didn't have to do that. I should be in jail right now." James wanted to reach out, touch her hand with his, but he kept them folded in his lap. He said he'd see her at the show. "But of course," he added, "please call if you need anything."

He wrote his number on a book of matches he took from the waitress.

*

He went to the show alone. His friend, Chris, was busy working another job.

He ordered coffee instead of beer.

The bartender dutifully informed James that the coffee there was shit.

He ordered anyway.

His drink was delivered in a dirty, glass mug. The bartender set a half-empty gallon of whole milk on the counter.

The coffee *was* shit.

James added the milk.

Stella took the stage around ten o'clock.

Her voice flooded his veins, chilled his bones. It was as though she'd been born there, finally returning home after an arduous journey.

James found her in the crowd after the set. They locked eyes, and she made her way through to him. A young man in a dark suit followed close behind. It looked as though Stella might be holding his hand, but James couldn't be certain. The man's ostentatious display of boredom and wavy hair and tattoos was a bit irritating. Stella introduced him as Ryan or Randy. James couldn't quite catch it, and didn't quite care. James and Stella chatted for a minute about nothing he could remember. He couldn't hear her over the noise.

Ryan or Randy put his lips too close to Stella's ear, lingered there for far too long. His hand was much too comfortable on her hip before he dissipated back into the crowd, leaving her with a smile much too wide.

Stella asked if James wanted to stick around for a drink. He raised his eyebrows, cocking his head to the side like the bartender had when he ordered that shit cup of coffee.

"I was gonna have a soda or something," she said. "Before I get out of here."

She was perfect silence and awkward conversations.

He stalled, stopped, and started again.

Stella forced a smile.

Heart racing, James kept shifting his weight from the right foot to the left and back again. He didn't know what to do with his hands. He wished he'd never had that cup of coffee. He could feel himself blushing, tried to make it stop. *How's a guy supposed to make a thing like that stop?* It was dark in the parking lot, the neon lights of the glowing bar sign hanging far enough behind them. Maybe Stella couldn't tell.

"Thanks for coming out to see the show," she said instinctively reaching out to touch his arm like she'd done to so many men so many times before. Then thinking better of it, she kept her hand where it was.

"You were incredible up there."

She smiled, but it wasn't forced. This time it was because sometimes it's nice to hear you are incredible.

Ryan or Randy stumbled out of the bar and into the night.

Stella looked down, at her shoes, at the gravel beneath them, at his shoes—James was wearing boots that made his feet look too big. She looked everywhere but his eyes. Even though she craved it, she couldn't handle compliments when she felt she didn't deserve them. She looked at the wound scabbing over on his forehead. "Did you...?"

"There's a...small bruise."

"On your brain?"

"It's nothing serious. I have to go back to the doctor next week for a check-up."

She told him she'd better get going.

"Yeah. Right. Okay. It's getting late." He had to piss, and couldn't remember what he'd just said. Hell. He had to get a hold of himself. She was only a girl. He'd talked to a hundred girls before.

That sinking feeling he was sinking into, he was sinking into her.

"Yeah, it is late. Well, goodnight," she said, finally looking into his eyes. And that thing she feared would happen, happened.

She felt safe.

James moved in for the hug. Stella accepted his embrace. She inhaled his scent. He smelled good. Really good. He was gentle, nice to look at. And there was the accident. They would forever have that. He'd been there for her. He smelled this way when he first held her in his arms. She had no real memory of that day, only fragments of moments constructed backwards and forwards: broken glass, ripped metal, and a heartbeat, slow and steady. His heartbeat. And that smell. Like he hadn't broken a sweat in all that mess. His life had been in her hands and she was oh, so careless.

Now he was there at her show. She only had to ask once. They barely knew each other, and he came without question. How many times had she asked Craig to come?

Craig never showed. Not once. Not ever.

There was a bottomless pit of loneliness you could feel in a crowded room when you didn't know a single soul. She'd been falling for far too long.

So she found herself telling him to call. "You know. If you want. Sometime. Maybe we could chat."

"Yeah," James agreed. They would chat. It might be nice.

They did. And it was.

Overreacting to every breath of intoxicated air still lingering in the room, James didn't know—couldn't have known—where Stella had gone.

A hundred and twenty minutes came and went without an urgency to be anywhere. His lip started to hurt like hell. His knuckles were swollen. He'd never punched anyone before. They were going to be twice the size in the morning, if morning would ever come.

After wasting thirty more minutes picking glass from his knees, he decided to race outside without shoes and without a shirt. The cold bit his skin and slowed his blood, but that didn't stop him from running, scanning the streets. He did laps around the block until he was certain she was gone.

*

She was summertime Sunday afternoons.

They picnicked in the park.

Her head in his lap, his hands through her dark, purple hair, Stella looked at James and squinted because she'd forgotten her sunglasses in the car.

"When are you going to marry me?" she asked.

"I can't marry you yet," he told her. "It's only been four months."

Stella's toes curled around the grass, bending and yanking the blades from the earth. "That's not good enough. What does four months have to do with anything?"

It was a hundred and ten degrees in the sun, but so, so cool in the shade.

"Everything," James replied.

"You're stalling."

"You're rushing."

"Don't you love me?" She tickled him. She attacked from the right, making him believe she'd go for that spot just below his ribs, but sent an unsuspecting hand up through the bottom of his shorts where she knew him to be most vulnerable. He never saw it coming.

They laughed. He grabbed her wrists, attempting to seize control, but she pinned him down and straddled his waist. The yellow summer dress she wore hiked its way up passed her knees. She pushed it down. He tried to sneak a peak and was swatted away.

Stella hated her knobby knees. James wanted to kiss them.

She brought her face close to his and whispered, "I want you always." She punctuated her sentence with a bite to his ear.

He couldn't marry her. Not yet. He couldn't give her the life he knew she deserved. He'd lost his construction job shortly after the accident, his boss claiming something about a diminished reaction time. "Someone could get seriously injured around here," his boss had said. Now what? Stella was all he had. He wasn't going to lose her too. She lived a lifetime of hurt and broken relationships. He saved her. From all of that. He was responsible for her now. James was determined to be the one to restore her hope in men.

Stella allowed his hands to make their way under her dress. Her head fell back, looking up into the tree for something that might have gotten stuck there.

"Not yet. But soon. I will marry you soon."

She looked down at him, his hands on her thighs and he got this far because he looked at her, *really* looked at her, and not at her knobby knees.

When his fingertips nipped the edge of her underwear, she pulled his hands free.

This will never be good enough would have to be good enough for now.

Three days came and went without word from Stella.

James was sick. His stomach cramped, his abdomen throbbed. He couldn't slouch. It hurt when he applied too much pressure to his left leg when he walked. His entire left side was going numb and throbbing.

The wound, he knew, was infected.

He hadn't gone to the doctor.

At least the swelling had gone down on his lips where her knuckles had split them. He'd taken the beating until Stella swung and missed, and shattered the bathroom mirror.

The sound of sleep still in her voice, Stella said good morning to James. The remnants of the night still in her green eyes, she tried to blink it away.

They spent their first night together four weeks after the show. Talking till three a.m., they fell asleep on his bed in their clothes.

She was on her stomach. James crawled over her, a tank top exposing bare shoulders; he kissed them. He kissed every inch of skin he could find. The pace of her breath quickened. Fingertips down her arms, palms pressed to the small of her back, he worked her shirt up over her head.

James couldn't keep a steady job since the construction company let him go. He'd stopped painting. His thoughts seemed to collide with one another. He would see an apple and call it pear, even though he knew the damn thing was an apple. He nearly lost his life for Stella, and she knew he would lay it down again in an instant. But she was the reason he sometimes got lost counting to ten, and couldn't remember the name of the street he lived on.

She'd never forgive herself.

*

Stella arrived at James's apartment to find it black, only illuminated by straining moonlight. She was curious to know why James was sitting in the dark. He was reluctant to tell her the electric company had shut everything off. He kissed her, gentle at first.

His hands were dark and stained. Stella smiled. He must have been painting. His face was smudged and blotted too. She loved watching him create. Her heart leapt at the hope that maybe, just maybe, he was finally getting better.

She needed him to be better.

The thought aroused her. She inadvertently touched herself.

James paced around the loft, running a hand through his overgrown hair while keeping his left hand firmly pressed to his abdomen as though he were trying to stop his insides from spilling out. "I'm in trouble," he said.

"What do you mean?" Stella stalled because she was there to tell him what she had done. What had happened the night of her show; the night of their first date.

"Financially."

She thought James was doing okay, and wanted to know why he hadn't told her.

I'm telling you about it now, he thought, but thought better of it and said he'd gotten a bit careless. He'd been spending too much money. He was careful with his words because what he really wanted to say was that he'd been spending too much money on her. Not that she demanded it, but she liked to be spoiled. And he wanted to spoil her.

"How did you let yourself get into this situation?" She then asked if there was a flashlight or something. "Maybe a candle?"

He did it for her. Would she understand that? Of course she would. She was his girl, and they were in this together.

"I got comfortable." James leaned against the counter. Stared at the floor. The pacing made him lightheaded. He needed to hurry this along. "Then I got nervous." He looked at her. Her eyes so bright they were headlights in a dark, dark world. "I want to marry you."

Stella kept searching for a flashlight.

He wanted to take a seat. Standing was really starting to wear him down. "I know things are tight right now. But I don't want to work in some office where they post motivational quotes from Einstein on cubical walls, and pictures of kittens hanging on tree branches." He wanted to raise his voice at her, but knew she'd cower away and he'd want to fight if it came to that. He would poke and prod her like a sleeping bear. When she awoke, they'd both regret it. No. He needed to remain calm. They needed to talk about this. Like adults. They were going to get married. They needed money. So he said, "Chris told me it was a sure thing."

Stella wanted to know what a "sure thing" was. She never liked Chris. She could tell he took advantage of James. She looked at his hands again. "Have you been painting? What are you working on? I'd love to see it." When they got inside, the money was right where Chris said it would be. He got that much right.

But Chris had also said the guy, Leo, wouldn't be home.

"No," James frowned.

"Then what's that all over your hands?"

James wanted to tell her what happened; that Leo *had* been home. And Leo had had a knife. He said, "I'm with you during all my free time. How can I paint when I am with you?"

"Do *not* put this on me."

Chris had abandoned him in the house. Leo's blade sunk into James's flesh, their bodies pressed together. The sickly breathe of rotting teeth heaving against James's neck. He hadn't felt a thing until he looked down saw the knife inside of him.

His knee reacted, jerked upward more out of shock than self-defense.

Stay focused, he thought. *Focus. Focus. Focus.* "I want to spend that time with you. I love you. I don't want to be without you. I don't care about anything else."

"Obviously you don't because your electricity is turned off." She flipped switches just to prove her point.

James lost his focus. "Maybe if I'd made you pay for the damages and bills from the accident, I wouldn't be in this fucking situation."

Skin on skin. Hard and loud. He spat on the floor, and was sure that was blood he tasted.

"Don't you *ever* talk to me like that," Stella whispered, lips quivering.

James dared not touch his cheek no matter how bad it burned. Dowse him in gasoline and light a match, and he wouldn't even try to put himself out.

Hand on forehead, Stella said she needed a drink.

"Yeah, that's it. There's the answer."

"I said I *need* a drink. I didn't say I was going to *have* one."

So instead of telling her he needed a doctor, James thought it was more important to ask: "Have you?"

"Have I what?"

The kind of silence that lays waste to logical thinking hung so thick in the air he was certain neither of them was getting out of there alive.

"Had a drink..." He could have taken a knife from the drawer and planted it neatly into her back, between the shoulder blades where she'd never be able to reach and yank it free. It would have been the same thing.

"Who the hell do you think you are?"

"I..."

"How can you even ask me that?"

A broken heart.

A lost cause.

A slamming door.

He chased her down in the hallway. Stella was in heels, and hadn't made it far. James grabbed at her wrist and oh, the awful way she recoiled, falling into the wall. He stumbled forward, trying to grab her again. They both collapsed at the top of the stairs.

"I don't even know what we're fighting about," she said, or maybe he said it.

James tried to comfort her, to calm her, tried to get his arms around her, but everything felt so awkward. The pain in his flesh was a searing, white-hot intensity.

Stella cried. She grew angry for crying. "I'm trying to be this person for you. This person I can't be. I don't know how to be her. I've changed so much for you. Over these months. So much. I don't know which pieces are the real me any more. I just want to be me. I'm so tired of the guilt. For what I've done to you."

They sat there at the top of those steps, holding each other for an hour not saying a word.

He bled quietly in the dark.

James still hadn't gone to the hospital. He tried to tend to the wound himself. He didn't have the stomach for stitches, so he bought butterfly bandages and gauze and endless amounts of creams and ointments. He swallowed painkillers every thirty minutes. And every time he made a wrong move, every time the pain shot through his stomach, clawed its way into his chest until it came tearing through his brain—temporarily blinding and rendering him helpless—he just had to think of the money.

He had gotten away with the money.

He was going to marry Stella.

The next day he bought the ring.

Everything was going to be okay.

"Of all the gin joints in all the world," is what Melissa said to James when she saw him at the bar. He'd been waiting for Stella. They were supposed to have met for their date over an hour ago.

She wasn't answering the phone. He wanted to trust her. But...he couldn't. Not anymore. Not after the way she reacted when he asked her about drinking. So he went to the bars. When he didn't find her, he took a seat and ordered a coffee to calm his nerves.

He couldn't stop thinking about the hole in his gut. Five days old and not looking any better. Maybe it was time to go to the doctor.

Melissa took up the seat next to him, her scent rendering his senses defenseless.

The bar was crowded. He hadn't recognized the smell until she got close. Too close.

"How long had it been?"

"Going on three years, I think." James knew. It would be three years next month.

Melissa mouthed the word, "Wow," and ordered a beer from the bartender. She nodded at the cup of coffee in front of him. "Not drinking anymore?"

"Not since the day I left you."

"Christmas Eve," she dutifully reminded him. "Left without a word."

James dug dirt out from beneath his fingernails. "You never got my letter?"

"You never sent a letter."

"I never could lie to you."

"And here you are," she continued. "The City of Angeles."

"Here I am," he echoed.

"I'm glad to see you're sober now."

The bartender delivered her beer.

James asked what Melissa was doing in town. She'd just moved. "A few weeks ago, actually."

They chatted about the good times living together in Pittsburgh, and the bad. It had been mostly bad. With his excessive drinking and her free-spirited nature. But when the times were good, damn, they were good. Somewhere amidst their discussion, a hand ended up on his knee.

He flinched, but didn't pull away.

James finished his drink, said he'd better be going. Melissa left him her number, kissed him on the cheek. Said it was really nice to see him, and hoped he would call.

The next bar, the bar where Stella always performed, was less crowded than the Lion and Fiddle where he'd run into Melissa.

Melissa. What were the odds?

James took a seat at the counter. The bartender hadn't seen Stella.

Defeated and more worried than ever, James stood to leave, bumping into someone behind him.

"Hey. Watch it, mate…"

James apologized and moved to be on his way.

"I know you. You're the boyfriend."

James stopped and turned. He recognized the man. "And you are?"

"Name's Rich," the Aussie shot out his free hand. "A friend of our dear Stella."

James nodded. Ryan or Randy's name was Rich. They shook hands. "Yes," he said, "I am indeed the boyfriend." Rich's grip was strong and confident. "Remind me, how did you meet Stella again?"

"Well, the same way you did, right? I just brought her home after the show..." Rich trailed off, stared deep into the beer remaining in his glass before swallowing the contents in one final gulp. Rich wiped his mouth with the back of his hand. "Have a good night, mate. I'd best be going."

"Wait. What? What was that?"

Pulling on his coat, Rich said, "You're the one she left me for."

"You two dated?" Roller coasters were easier to handle than hearing this.

"Fucked a lot. Made love. Whatever you want to call it."

James felt nauseous. Sick to his very core.

"I met her the night I met you." He patted his new friend on the shoulder. "The things that girl will do..."

James hit Rich, and felt Rich's cheekbone collapse and disintegrate upon impact.

He left the bar without looking back, before the police could get there, and called Melissa.

The skin an inch or more in every direction around the puncture wound had turned black with tiny flecks of green and yellow and purple splattered through like a rotten Pollock imitation.

James had taken to throwing up once a day. The stomach pains were made of something crippling.

He regretted not having gone to the hospital. But what could he say if he went there now? There would be too many questions and not enough answers. He had to tough it out.

He hadn't seen Stella in two weeks. He had himself convinced she was drinking again. That she must be back with Rich. This caused a whole new hurt in his gut.

He still hadn't cleaned up the bathroom mirror.

James pulled a jacket on over his t-shirt and jeans. With his hands in the pockets, he wrapped it close to his body to keep from shivering. Outside it was good to feel the bitter November air sting his face.

Everything had to go. All James could see was Stella and Rich in the backseat of her car, in her bed, the very bed they shared. He could hear her whimpering. Her short, quick breath. He saw Rich's hands tender against her breasts, sliding between her legs.

James collapsed on the stairs leading to his apartment, overwhelmed and destructively anxious. Had Stella liked it? He wanted so badly for it not to be true. He worked up the courage to go inside, and made it to the sink in time to vomit.

He could still smell Melissa on his hands.

"Oh Lord," he kept thinking. *"What have I done?"*

Stella called his name over the running water pouring from the faucet, his insides rinsing down the drain. When James entered the bedroom, she threw her arms around him. He haphazardly kissed her, tasting tequila and stale cigarettes. She pulled away. "Have you been drinking?"

What was she taking about? She was the one with the drinking problem.

She wanted to know where James had been. She tried to remind him they planned to stay in that night. Did he not remember?

Was it was getting worse? Maybe *he* was the one who'd gotten confused.

Stella asked what was wrong.

"I was waiting for you…"

"Where?"

"I called. You never answered."

James was holding his phone. Stella took it from his hand. She looked at the call history, and held the phone up to his face. "This isn't my number. None of these are. You were calling the wrong number. Are you okay?"

"Am I okay? Am I okay? You slept with Rich."

Stella's body went cold and rigid. "What are you talking about? How do you…?"

"Don't."

"I think we need to take you to the doctor. You can tell me, did you have a drink?"

"How long?"

"How long? How long what?"

"How long were you sleeping together?"

Silence. Then: "That was before you," she whispered.

"That was the same night as me."

James called Melissa after macerating Rich's face. He hadn't intended to do anything. He should have gone right home. Melissa had already gone back to her apartment. He met her there. He apologized to her for the man he'd been when they were together. He thought that was why he'd gone to her place. To tell her he was sorry. She hugged him. Told him how much she missed him. Three years was a long time to invest in someone. Melissa kissed his check. He kissed her ear. She bit his neck. He worked the button on her jeans.

"And you've been drinking," James said, "I could taste it when I kissed you." He could still taste it. Then said something about Melissa, but couldn't remember. Maybe it was just in his head.

"Who's Melissa? You've been a completely different person this last week." Stella told him she was still sober. Sober since the day she got out of the hospital. "Look at me. What makes you think I've been drinking? Why don't you trust me? And who is Melissa?"

He wanted to say he was sorry, but right then he wasn't. He shouted back, "Why don't I trust you? Here's why. Stop avoiding it and just admit you fucked Rich instead of going home with me that night!"

She hit him until he bled then hit him some more.

A mirror shattered.

She collapsed.

He told her to get out.

She had nowhere to go.

He didn't care. He couldn't stand the sight of her. Couldn't stand himself.

Stella left.

Oh, Lord, he thought again after she'd gone. *Oh, Lord, what have I done?*

James stood on the steps of Stella's apartment, sweating even though he was freezing. He waited out front. He sat outside until one of the residences from the complex came home with a bag of groceries. He slipped in behind them. He climbed the four flights of stairs, and found the door unlocked. He could feel the bile rising.

He knocked.

A man James did not recognized answered, and he greeted this intruder by hitting him in the face. The man recoiled, hands to nose, blood seeping between fingers. James pushed passed him into the apartment. He went for the bedroom and found Stella there, getting dressed.

"You're here," she said.

"I'm here."

"Where's Greg?"

"Look me in the eyes and tell me you don't love me."

"What are you talking about?"

"Tell me you never want to see me again. Just tell me, and I'll go."

"Are you okay?"

He screamed it this time. "TELL ME YOU FEEL NOTHING!"

Stella looked as though James had just hit her and not Greg. Wind swept in through the open windows, carrying with it the sound of life.

"I don't love you," she said. She whispered it. "I can't. I look at you and only see my mistakes. I'm sorry."

He threw up right there on the carpet, dropping to his knees in just enough time for the bat to miss his head and shatter the bedside lamp.

Stella screamed.

"How could you be with someone else already?" James gagged.

Greg geared up for another swing. Stella grabbed his wrists and begged him to stop.

She went to the floor, cradling James. He was sweating with the profuse efficiency of a fever. She touched his stomach, felt the color red.

"I'd have died for you," he said. "I still would."

Greg lowered the bat.

"Call an ambulance," Stella instructed.

Greg hesitated.

"Call an ambulance. CALL AN AMBULANCE!" She had to shout it before Greg dropped the bat and left the room.

"I'm so sorry," she whispered. "You're going to be okay." She said it over and over again, combing his wet hair with her fingers. "You're going to be okay." She removed his coat to press it against the wound. She found the box in his pocket.

She opened it.

She cried.

*

Everything was white. A vacuum in deep space. All sound and color had been sucked out of existence. There was glass. James found that first. Tiny pebbles of glass everywhere like an entire sack of rocks and marbles had been dumped into his lap, down his shirt, over his head.

Formless shapes filling in with recognizable colors manifested against the white. Sounds, distant noises muffled like he was underwater, just below the surface, running out of air.

He was at the wheel of his car. The windshield blown. The windows gone. His seatbelt still on, slicing through his neck and collarbone. He unhooked the buckle, felt the fabric of the belt peel away with skin. A neat layer of white residue, almost like snow, collected on every surface and drifted about the interior of the vehicle. The airbags had torn the dashboard to pieces.

The driver's side door caved inward. James threw his weight into it, pulling on the handle until it opened barely wide enough for him to squeeze through. He collapsed onto hot pavement into unstructured puddles of glass. He cried out, tiny knives slicing their way in wherever they could.

The air was all smoke and burning rubber.

Someone shouting: "Are you okay?"

Someone shouting: "Don't move!"

"You've been hit," a voice told him. "By that truck." James followed the finger belonging to the voice pointing at the truck now halfway inside the convenience store located on the corner of the intersection. The driver had sped right through the red light.

"Stay where you are. We've called 911."

James forced himself off the street. Right hand on left arm. On his knees. On his feet. He took two steps and collapsed.

"Has anyone checked on the guy in the store?"

"Where are the police?"

"Is anyone else hurt?"

James's car sat in the middle of the intersection. He absorbed the scene in just enough time to watch another vehicle smash into what was left of his car. It spun out of control, colliding with the pickup truck on the sidewalk. The crash sent the pickup forward, completing its entrance into the store, bringing down the glass walls forming the establishment. The third vehicle fresh on the scene came to a destructive halt against the brick of a neighboring building.

Back on his feet, James ran into the store. He slipped in a pool of gasoline and antifreeze and Pepsi.

The smoking engines activated the alarm system. The sprinklers turned on.

A young girl was half out of the pickup, the driver's door hanging on its last hinge, creaking every so slightly back and forth, back and forth. She was caught on the seatbelt, hanging there, completely vulnerable. James dropped to his knees in the middle of a full on run, sliding through busted bags of potato chips and M&M's.

Her black and purple shirt wet with blood. The right side of her face broken and ruptured. Her eye. He was certain she'd lost her eye.

He asked if she was okay.

He shouted the words.

He heard others shouting too.

He heard sirens.

He grabbed the girl's wrist, but could feel no pulse. He wasn't certain how to check for a thing like that anyway. He reached across her lap and unhooked the seatbelt, her thin, frail body slumping lifeless into his. He fell back to the floor, crashing against a rack of red wine. He could feel her chest moving.

She was still alive. But for how long?

She smelled of Red Bull and cheap vodka.

Purple hair knotted through his fingers, he wiped the blood from her face, out of her eyes.

Her purple lips and a sick, sinking feeling in his gut.

"You're going to be okay," he said over and over again as slow and calm as he could. "You're going to be okay."

We Can't Go Home Again

ABOUT THE AUTHOR

Max Andrew Dubinsky lives on the road and sometimes in California. His writing has been published with *Relevant Magazine, People of the Second Chance, The Good Men Project*, and he is the author/creator of the online, serialized novel experience, *Dislocated*. He blogs at MakeItMAD.com, and fears sharks in all water situations. This is his first book.

Twitter: @maxdubinsky

Made in the USA
Lexington, KY
06 July 2012